Christmas 1992

To Tyrone,

FURTHER CONFESSIONS

Probably nothing in comparison
to your own — they'd likely
make your hair curl ... Eek!
Check out the mirror!
  Told you so!

    Peace be with you,

      Love and hamsters,

          Bob :)
            xxx

Also available

CONFESSIONS
Simon Mayo

SNOGGING
Simon Mayo and Martin Wroe

FURTHER CONFESSIONS

More secrets from the Radio 1 FM
Breakfast Show Confessional

SIMON MAYO

Marshall Pickering
An Imprint of HarperCollins*Publishers*

Marshall Pickering is an Imprint of
HarperCollins*Religious*,
Part of HarperCollins*Publishers*,
77–85 Fulham Palace Road, London W6 8JB

First published in Great Britain
in 1992 by Marshall Pickering

1 3 5 7 9 10 8 6 4 2

A catalogue record for this book is
available from the British Library

ISBN 0 551 02656 1

Printed and bound in Great Britain by
HarperCollins*Manufacturing* Glasgow

CONTENTS

For my parents

INTRODUCTION

Aliens wasn't as good as *Alien*. The *Godfather Part 2* was not as stunning as the *Godfather*, and *Rocky 2, 3, 4, 5 and probably by now 6* and *7*, were not as exciting as *Rocky 1* (a difficult feat admittedly). Sequels rarely surpass the original, but this book, I think, modestly, breaks the rule. All the confessions in this book are monsters. These are the ones we get calls, letters and memos about. These are the tales that have probably been party pieces for years. These are the confessions that make people late for work and school every morning.

There are some of course that will never be broadcast or printed. This is a shame because I've got a great Japser Carrot story, an unbelievable monastery story, and a government-shaking ministerial scandal. But they'll keep. (Volume 3?)

Thanks as ever go to Dianne, Rod, and Ric who gasp, laugh, whoop and howl through our daily forgiveness exercise. Also to the BBC duty officers who face the telephonic flak as another dead budgie bites the dust.

And thanks to you for getting the joke.

MATTHEW CHAPTER 6 VERSES 14 & 15

1

Little Darlings

The most often used excuses for what is, frankly, the appalling behaviour exhibited in the confessions I receive, are drink and youth. Drink we'll come to later, as I'm sure did the parents of the little blighters of whom you are about to read.

They say the first sixteen years are the worst . . .

Dear Father Mayo,
Bless me Father, for I wish to confess my sins, or rather the sins of my sister.

Seventeen years ago when my sister was a young and innocent girl she decided to be naughty and go in search of her Christmas presents in Mum and Dad's bedroom. During the search she found a large box that looked suspiciously as though it might be a present – but it wasn't. On opening it she discovered it was in fact an enormous economy pack of condoms. The thought of my Dad buying in bulk and being such a cheapskate with it made her change her present hunt into a vindictive few moments of sabotage. She found a needle and stuck it through each condom packet giving it a wiggle for good measure.

The result of such a frenzied attack of disgust is sitting here writing this letter to you, and I was wondering if my sister Sally could ever, ever, ever be forgiven? Could I also possibly have forgiveness of her for blabbing this because I swore I wouldn't but I couldn't resist?

Yours,
from the sperm that got away!

Dear Father Mayo,

My confession dates back to the days of decimalization when I was only a wee young lad. Being a very inquisitive and daft child, I did what everyone of my age would have done with a new 2p piece – I swallowed it!

After the initial panic of turning blue and the apparent lack of breath, I calmed myself down and decided to seek help. I rushed home and told my mother, who insisted on a trip to the local hospital. Sitting in the waiting room, with children with saucepans on their heads and buttons stuck up their noses (just the usual, quite normal day at Sunderland General Hospital) I awaited my fate.

After what seemed hours I was taken into a room with more gadgets than the Star Ship Enterprise and asked to undress and lie on the table. 'Don't worry son, I'm only giving you an X-ray,' explained the doctor. 'It won't hurt a bit and is completely safe,' he said as he hurried behind a lead wall.

A few minutes later he announced what I already knew, 'You've swallowed a 2p piece.' 'Amazing', I thought. What will we have to do?' asked my worried mother'. 'No surgery is required' the doctor replied. 'Just let nature take its course'. It wasn't until I got home that I was informed what that meant. From then on I had to do the obvious in a bucket until the 2p was found, a job my mother thought best suited to . . . dad! For nearly two weeks he searched the contents of the bucket, sometimes twice a day, until the 2p was finally discovered, much to his relief.

Now after all these years I have decided to confess all. I have never had the heart, or guts, to come clean and admit that I found the 2p on the same day I returned from the hospital and decided to plant a 2p in the bucket when I could see dad had had enough. Can you forgive me for this dreadful deed?

Will my dad forgive me?

Will the Royal Mint forgive me?

Please end my suffering as I can't look at a 2p piece without filling with guilt.

Yours Owning-up-ingly,
Gary
(Age 25¾)!!

Dear Father Mayo,
The time has come to unburden my troubled mind.

Let me take you back several years to my childhood, and one blissful summer spent at the east coast. To get away from the madding crowds, my parents took me to a little-known stretch of beach called Blackhouse. With childlike curiosity I asked why no one else was on the beach, only to have my father explain it was a bombing range used by the RAF. Apparently, his father used to bring the horse and cart onto the beach, collecting bombs to use as weights for holding the tarpaulins over haystacks.

Encouraged by this tale I set out to find a bomb of my own. Imagine my surprise when by chance I happened upon one. Full of glee I struggled (as it was heavy) back to my parents with the prize. When time came to leave the beach and conclude the holiday, the bomb came too. It found a home in the garden shed, where in times of boredom I clouted it with a sledge hammer and chisel in a vain attempt to discover its contents.

About a year later we moved house and district. It was my task to clear the shed. Tired of the bomb which had lost its appeal, I put it into a cardboard box with some old paint tins. Dad and I took the box to the scrap-yard and I was pleased with the coppers it earned. Imagine my surprise, the following day, when the local paper arrived, with the headline 'Toff sells scrapman a bomb'. Apparently the scrapman had been curious as to why the box was so heavy, he tipped out the contents to reveal the answer . . .

I would like to beg forgiveness from the frightened scrapman, the police, fire brigade, all the residents of the vicinity of the scrapyard who were evacuated, and the bomb squad who were called to defuse the offending article.

Yours sincerely,
Ned.

Dear Father Mayo,

I was listening to your confession spot at work this morning, and I feel I must now confess to the mean rotten thing that I did to my father when I was the tender age of seven.

Whilst he was having his Sunday afternoon nap, I was terribly bored – like one normally is on Sunday – when I suddenly spotted my felt-tip pens lying on the floor. I decided to be artistic and proceeded to colour-in my father's bald patch with an array of colours.

Nobody spotted this until the next afternoon when he was at work. He was chairing an important meeting, and wondered why everybody sniggered when he bent down to refer to his notes. It wasn't until coffee break that one of them kindly pointed out that he had what looked like a rainbow on his head. I don't know how he managed to hide his embarrassment for the rest of the day, but he came home in a foul mood and grounded me, my brother and sister for the rest of the week as no one would admit to it.

I would like now to apologize to my brother and sister, for, due to this, we all had to miss a party we had been looking forward to for a long time.

I hope you will forgive me.

Love from Pandora.

Dear Simon and All,

I've carried my confession for many years and now finally I feel it's time to reveal all and rid me of my sins!

We were moving house. Everything was carefully packed into boxes and stored in our dining room. As my parents were out at the time, I decided to ask a friend round to play, but after she came round we became bored and restless as all of my games had been packed away and out of reach. That's when we decided to raid the kitchen cupboards. We found nothing exciting except an 'Angel Delight', so feeling quite hungry we whipped the mix up as fast as we could. Mum could have walked in at any second.

When we had finished mixing, the pudding still looked rather boring. That's when I had a great idea! I could remember seeing some Hundreds and Thousands in a box right at the back of all the items my parents had already packed. I quickly hurried to the box and pulled them out. As I did, the lid came off and out flew hundreds and thousands of the Hundreds and Thousands!

In a panic I shouted at my friend to go and stall my mother (who was due back at any moment) while I tidied up. As I was hoovering and struggling round the boxes with my arms going frantically everywhere, I heard a ripping sound. Slowly I looked round and a wave of horror swept over me. In my panic to tidy up I had put the end of the hoover through the canvas of my parents prized painting they had bought while living in Singapore.

I finished hoovering and for the rest of the day was a nervous wreck. All night I prayed my parents wouldn't notice their favourite painting had been defaced (they didn't!). The next day after school I took it down to the nearest field and threw it as far as I could into someone's garden.

A few weeks later we moved to our new house and after several days of unpacking I overheard my dad asking my mum where she had put the painting. She said that she didn't know, but she definitely remembered the removal man putting it into his van. After several hours of searching for it my dad was on the phone to the removal company saying he would never use them again and that he would refuse to pay his bill. He even threatened to go and see a solicitor. The Removal Company took details of our move and said the matter would be dealt with and the driver reprimanded.

Meanwhile, I sat in the dining room listening to the conversation with a smug grin on my face. For a moment I felt sorry for the removal van driver, and how with my help he was one step nearer the dole queue.

But now the time has come to ask for forgiveness from my parents, for I demolished their prized picture and also to the removal man, who swore on his life he never took it.

Do you forgive me?

A. Nonymous

Simon,

Bless me father, for I have sinned . . . I have to confess to something I did over Christmas.

For ages my mother had been nagging my father about all the old cine films that he has accumulated over the past 30-odd years – clips of their wedding, *all* my sisters' and my birthday parties, our family, friends and pets too!

Almost anything any of us did he would have to film it. The films were in such a mess that dad decided, as a Christmas surprise for mum, he'd have them all transferred on to VHS video cassettes. Twenty-odd messy tapes soon condensed down into two neat modern ones. Great!

Christmas Eve, my father gathered mum, my sister and I into the lounge to watch him throw all the old tapes onto the big open fire. Mum went into a state of shock, while all dad could do was smile and say 'Wait until tomorrow'!

Christmas Day arrived and my mother was over the moon (and relieved) with her present. But, with this being a rather busy time of year with plenty of good films on TV, we never got round to watching them.

It wasn't until January that I decided to watch a few things I had videoed over the festive season. First of all I put on the film *Dirty Dancing* followed by several clips of *Top of the Pops*. Then, to my horror, I noticed a rather familiar face on the screen. It was my 28-year-old sister celebrating her fifth birthday. This only lasted a few seconds then the tape ended.

I felt sick. I scrambled about, praying the second 'Family Memories' tape was still OK.

As I pushed it into the machine and pressed 'play', the same 'I might as well just kill myself now' feeling filled my body, as Henry and Madge Ramsey came up on the screen, followed by the TV show *Blind Date*, and other rather important things of equal interest. Thirty years of family history gone!!

My parents have not yet discovered what's happened. If it's any consolation . . . Mum and Dad, you are better dancers than Patrick Swayze and Jeniffer Warne, and big sis, you look better with your clothes on and no potty on your head!

Am I forgiven?

Elisha.

Dear Simon,

I have decided to confess my darkest secret.

My family originate from Sheffield. I am the eldest of three sisters and life was reasonably happy for my next sister down and me until one fateful 18th July, when our youngest sister, Anne arrived. She was the child who everyone who gazed into her pram exclaimed, 'Isn't she beautiful'.

Now this carried on throughout her babyhood, whilst she was a toddler, a mixed infant and through her junior school (still carries on to this day Simon actually). As you might imagine, my other sister and I grew mighty fed up with all this adulation of our youngest sister, but it wasn't until Anne reached the age of about 12 or 13 that we successfully managed to plot our revenge. Our revenge revolved around her being asleep, darkness and a bottle of trick tan (the sort that makes you go orange overnight).

The plan was hatched. When Anne went to sleep (for someone so beautiful she didn't half snore like a pig) my sister and I smeared her face, arms and hands with fake tan. Next morning when she woke up she made her usual trip to the mirror to admire the perfect reflection and screamed in horror when she saw her face all blotchy and brown – not to mention the arms and hands attractively patterned to match. Our parents were called and were suitably horrified while my other sister and I had to feign our shock whilst trying incredibly hard not to laugh (revenge is so sweet not to mention hysterically funny).

Well, baby sister was dispatched to the doctor who could see no reason for the strange skin pigmentation. Our campaign carried on for some months with each recurrence of the blotches more baffling than the previous attack. In short Simon, I would now like to apologize to my sister Anne, our family doctor, and to the skin specialist at the Northern General Hospital.

No, it wasn't some strange skin condition – it was me, my sister Anne and a bottle of Tanfastic. Can we be forgiven?

Yours sincerely,
Claudia.

Dear Simon,

I must confess to something that has been with me for 18 years.

I was aged 11 and I arrived home from school one day in proud possession of two large magnets a friend had ripped out of the back of two old and very big Hi-Fi speakers. On arriving home my brother, three years my senior, told me about a wonderful experiment he had done in his physics class several weeks earlier.

Our television set was no more than a few days old. The black-and-white one had been playing up, so at great expense, Dad had gone out and bought the very latest all-singing-all-dancing colour TV set. They were still a bit of a novelty so ours was treated with the greatest of respect . . . until now!

My brother showed me, how to distort and jump the picture using my strong magnets. It was fantastic. Peter Purvis and the whole *Blue Peter* crew jumped and bent themselves all out of shape, changing colour like chameleons. We squealed with delight as our heroes proceeded to look so stupid.

After the fun had calmed down, we noticed the TV hadn't. We switched it on and off, changed channels, even the *Magpie* lot on the other side were all wrong!

We switched the telly off and listened to the radio and awaited Dad. He arrived home and went insane. We pleaded our innocence, claiming 'it just went like that when we switched it on'! He then interrogated us individually to see if our stories tallied. Fortunately they did.

The TV repair man was called. The day before he arrived, mysteriously the set fixed itself but he came to check it out anyway. 'It's OK,' he said, 'these models sometimes do that, when they're settling in' (winking at me and my brother). Needless to say my Dad sent the television back and never bought another of that make again.

Sorry Dad, you weren't going insane, it *was* me and my brother.

Are we forgiven?

Cheers mate . . . ,
Craig.

Dear Simon,

When I was aged 17 I worked for a small but up-and-coming Advertizing Agency. Times were hard and business was very slow. Things were looking very bleak when suddenly my company was asked to devise a large advertising campaign for a multinational company.

This was the break our company needed and we slaved for three months to produce artwork and ideas for the final presentation. The clients would visit regularly to see how the work was progressing and my boss was told that out of all the agencies competing for the vast account we had the most imaginative ideas and the account could only go to us.

As the deadline for the presentation to the clients grew nearer my boss, who was a constant chain smoker, became more and more worked up. On the morning of the presentation I decided to play a joke on him just to take his mind off what was a very important day. I obtained a box of exploding tips you put into cigarettes – the sort that go bang and blacken the face of the smoker – just for a laugh I might add.

I waited for my boss to go out of the room and while he was gone I just had time to take out one cigarette from his packet left on the desk. I crammed this cigarette with four exploding tips, not just one as

22

recommended. I thought this would be more fun. I replaced the packet on the desk and waited to see what would happen.

My boss returned, picked up the packet and went about his business. I chuckled to myself all morning as he smoked another and yet another cigarette, but nothing happened. With all the preparation taking place for the final presentation to our main client at 2.00 pm I forgot all about it.

The presentation went very well and the clients loved the new advertizing campaign. As they laughed and joked about the special relationship they wanted with our agency my boss produced a packet of cigarettes from his pocket. He offered one to the company's Managing Director. I really wanted to stop my boss from lighting it for him, but I didn't want to look stupid. As he took the lighter away there was a massive bang. Bits of tobacco flew across the room. The client sat stunned with the tip of the cigarette hanging from his mouth. His face was black with soot and his expensive suit turned from cream to grey.

My boss sat there too, with sheer horror on his face and the look of a man who was about to lose everything. I can't repeat the conversation they had after that, but it started with 'you silly b——r'. The clients stormed out of the room and all of the hard work we had done went down the drain.

It was lucky my boss blamed his 12-year-old son for the unfortunate incident. It was very unlucky for his son who got a good hiding, couldn't go out for a month and had his school trip to Italy cancelled.

If it's any consolation, I was made redundant a month later due to lack of work. Please forgive me. I have never played a practical joke since and am now a hard-working Hotel Manager.

Yours faithfully,
John Smith.

Dear Father Simon,

My burden is weighing me down – please hear my confession.

It happened this time last year when my sister had just returned from living in Italy for two years, and had taken a job in an old folks' home. This job was not her first choice, but she thought she'd stick with it until a better one came along. She'd been a care assistant for just over a month – doing all of those lovely jobs like retrieving false teeth from under the bed, when she finally managed to get an interview for a tele-sales job which was just what she'd been waiting for.

However, the bad news was that her interview had been arranged for a day where she was due to work at the old folks' home. Being a coward, she didn't have the nerve to phone her boss and say she wanted the day off, so she set about persuading me to 'be her' and phone up the miserable geezer and make up some excuse about why she wasn't coming in to work. If I did this for her – my sister said she would undertake the washing up for the next three months and let me wear anything in her wardrobe.

I thought this was a pretty good deal, so when the day came for her interview I settled down to make the phone call. Now, I have a short fuse which can ignite at any time – and what happened next was not intended at all.

When I phoned the rest home I was put through to my sister's boss. 'Hello this is Fiona – I'm sorry that I won't be coming into work today, but I tripped over the cat and I've blacked my eye and can't see out of it.'

There was a 10-second pause – then my sister's boss proceeded to tell me in no uncertain terms that it just wasn't good enough for I was lazy and good for nothing and had better get into work at once or face the consequences! This was just too much for my short fuse. No one calls me – or my sister – names, so I proceeded to tell him just what to do with his job and ended by telling him to stick his head in a commode.

My sister returned from her interview, confident she'd got the job – but the problem was she wouldn't know for sure for another month and was going to continue to work at the rest home until then. Had I phoned her boss?? What had he said??? Ermm . . . yes, I had – erm . . . he said to rest today – and hoped she'd be better tomorrow.

This is why she couldn't understand what was going on the next day when she arrived for work to find her P45 on the table with a curt note from her boss terminating her employment on the grounds of her unreasonable behaviour. She returned home in tears – and I did my level best to act surprised and outraged on her behalf. To this day she believes she lost her job because he found out she'd taken the day off to go for another interview.

I've been racked with guilt since then and would like to beg her forgiveness. I'm afraid I won't do a thing about the agreement over the dishes – and I enjoyed wearing her clothes. Oh, she did get the tele-sales job – but was unemployed for a month until she heard for sure – so I apologize for that too.

Sharon.

Dear Father Simon,

Forgive me, for I have sinned. My confession goes back to the early 1970s when I started work as a Junior Medical Secretary at Tameside General Hospital (then Ashton General Hospital).

I was straight from school, a young teenager who knew it all – you know the type. Well, as teenagers frequently do, I would argue with my Mum and be thoroughly obnoxious and storm off out to work. As the day wore on, I would begin to feel guilty about the argument and would arrive home with a beautiful bunch of flowers for my Mum and profuse apologies – until next time!

My Mum would receive many bunches of flowers – gladioli, roses, chrysanths, tulips, daffodils, carnations, even orchids – bought as she thought from my meagre salary. I have never had the heart to tell her that those lovely flowers – bought from my meagre salary – came, in fact, from the mortuary!

Am I forgiven?

Yours sincerely,
June.

Holloway
(Not H M Holloway)

To my Mum,

Remember when we first moved to London and you took us window shopping, and I, a mere slip of a child, stole that gyroscope from W. H. Smiths? You caught me and made me take it back.

To say I was sorry, I got you those neat pan cleaners, well I nicked those from Waitrose! Forgive me Mum and think of me when you do the dishes.

Ira.

2

Irresistible Temptations

In an old US comedy series called, I think, *The Bickersons*, the less–than–gifted wife, Blanche, always offered the same excuse when she'd upset her long suffering husband. Whether she'd smashed the car, upset the neighbours, or just spent too much money, she would always wail 'The Devil made me do it!' This chapter is dedicated to the fiend in all of us.

Dear Simon,

I have a confession to make concerning my wife, Hilary. For years she has prided herself on being a bit of a Nanette Newman when it comes to conserving washing up liquid, you know the brand that's kind to hands and rhymes with hairy. If Nanette can wash two tower blocks of dishes, I am sure my wife can wash three.

Well, the latest record to date is 10 weeks from a regular-sized bottle of the green stuff and she is still going strong. She's told all her friends and converted all the family to buy this amazing long-lasting liquid for she's absolutely convinced one bottle can go so far.

Now for the guilty bit. For at least the past six weeks I have been topping it up every night when she has gone to bed and I'm switching off lights and buttoning the place up before going to bed.

Just as a little twist, on the next bottle I am going to do the opposite – taking out the liquid every night. She won't know what has happened when she goes four days on a bottle and it's empty.

Yours faithfully,
Roger.

Dear Father Mayo,

I was a mere boy of 16, 25 years ago, when, to earn some extra money for Christmas, I signed on at the village Post Office to help with the Christmas mail.

The work started at 4 am each morning and initially involved sorting the mail into pigeon holes for each street and district. Now the hall where this work was carried out was very cold, despite the odd archaic gas heater, and so my number one priority job was to ensure there was a steady availability of hot tea.

While the regular postmen drank their tea they all seemed to have an endless supply of sandwiches, cakes and biscuits. As I hadn't had any breakfast I was extremely envious – not to mention hungry.

However, as I was sorting out my batch of mail, which incidentally seemed to contain all the 'Dear Santa' mail much to the regulars' delight, I noticed that one of the packages had not been wrapped too well. Further examination revealed the package to be a Chocolate Selection Pack. I immediately repaired the package and placed it in the appropriate pigeon hole. But earlier I had vigorously shaken the package causing a Mars bar to fall out.

You can imagine my dilemma – to re-open the package and risk causing further damage or to dispose of the item in a safe manner. I decided on the latter option.

Now, if there is one thing better than a nice hot cup of tea and a Mars bar at 5 am, it's a packet of Treats and a pint of milk freshly removed from a front doorstep at 6.30 am as one saunters around with the Christmas rush mail. And, if there is one thing better than a drink of milk and a packet of Treats, it's another nice cup of tea and a Bounty at 10 am prior to the second postal delivery.

You would be surprised at the number of Selection Packs and Christmas Stockings sent through the mail and how easily they become damaged. However, only one item ever fell out of any one package.

So I would like to beg forgiveness from any child who received a damaged Selection Pack with one item less than specified, to all the people who had disputes with their milkmen over the number of milk bottles left on their steps (especially to the nice lady who gave me a Christmas tip), to anyone who had a calendar pushed through their letter box folded in two (this was to disprove the theory that Calendars Do Not Bend) and, last but not least, to Her Britannic Majesty, Queen Elizabeth II, for eating the Royal Mail.

Regards,
Michael.

Dear Father Simon,

It is with mixed feelings that I write my true confession – I beg not only your forgiveness, but also that of a young, hopeful entertainer whose career was snuffed out at the very beginning.

It all happened on a Monday evening in December 1973 when I was a teacher at a large comprehensive school in Bognor Regis. Together with several other members of staff I was watching Hughie Green's Opportunity Knocks on TV at my flat. It was not my favourite show – but that night something magical happened. One of the acts that appeared was the worst performer any of us had seen – a dustman from Slough called Harold Gumm, with his wonder dog, Jack. He gave a monologue about standing in his back garden and hearing the cows in the distance (Moo, he went) then the pigs (Oink Oink) and the ducks (you've guessed – Quack Quack). He then whistled the tune of 'In a Monastery Garden' and finished by yodelling – at which point wonder dog Jack leapt into his arms and howled and howled.

We were howling with laughter – how could anything so bad be on TV? If it could be on once – couldn't it happen again? One of our group said he knew that to win Opportunity Knocks you only needed about 700 votes – fewer still at Christmas.

And so the plot was hatched. With 2,700 students at the school and a staffroom of over 200 people – many were straight from college and still had student friends all over the country, we could get Harold Gumm back – this time as the winner of Opportunity Knocks! And so it was that, with a political background of several General Elections, I headed the campaign team to get Harold Gumm back again.

That night was spent planning the campaign – phone calls to friends throughout the country telling them to vote for Harold Gumm, the school librarian agreed to prepare voting slips, other members of staff were contacted, we met at The Lamb at Pagham to finalize the next day's launch. In the morning during Tutorial periods the classes of the conspirators were informed. Soon the kids spontaneously produced posters and the school was bedecked with vote for Harold Gumm banners – there was even a campaign song, sung to the William Tell theme – 'Harold Gumm, Harold Gumm we will vote for him – Harold Gumm, Harold Gumm we will make him win. Ho' (Clenched first in the air).

Seven days passed – it was standing room only at the flat when Hughie Green announced the result – pandemonium broke out – Harold Gumm had won! But now we had to get him to win again. This week's performance was worse than the first – he had obviously used up his best material – a Jumbo jet flying over Heathrow was substituted for the cows, a ships siren for the pigs – but wonder dog Jack still performed well!

The campaign swung into action – Harold Gumm won again – only to have his reign cut short by Christmas, and then a change in the rules for voting. Perhaps Hughie Green had sussed us for Harold Gumm was never to appear again. Until two years ago.

Here I must crave real forgiveness. We had made the British public endure the worst TV performance ever (until the 1990 Brit awards), we had abused Hughie Green, we had raised Harold Gumm's expectation of stardom – but in doing all this, we had also reduced a great British entertainer to tears of desolation, disappointment and despair – for Harold Gumm had beaten into second place none other than Su Pollard. She had to endure years of obscurity – eventually to emerge in Hi de Hi – beaten by Harold Gumm, Wonder Dog Jack and the Bognor Regis school.

Forgive me father, forgive me Su Pollard, I knew not what I was doing.

John.

Dear Father Mayo,

We feel the time has come to confess all, the burden of guilt has finally overwhelmed us one and all!!

We are a bunch of rather bored insurance clerks. The offices in which we earn a crust are next door to a rather large supermarket, where we spend many a fun-packed lunchtime. It is also where our dastardly crime was committed.

The pressure of all this inactivity finally began to tell, so we decided to try and relieve the boredom with a small and harmless practical joke. It was a Wednesday lunchtime. The four of us were standing conspicuously by the supermarket entrance and by golly we were prepared. Neil had a stopwatch, Peter a clipboard, while Richard and Eddie clutched a bunch of flowers for our lucky winner.

After several minutes our victim wandered unsteadily into the market and by coincidence it was a small, frail, bemused old lady. The conversation went something like this:

Neil, Eddie, Peter and Richard – 'Congratulations!!!! You're our millionth customer of the year You've won a free three-minute trolley

36

dash. Stuff as much loot as you can in this trolley and you take it all home free.'

Over the frail face came an expression of joy and determination. Off she went. It was a marvellous sight, such enthusiasm in one so old. She shot along the aisle like a bullet from a gun, stuffing packets of cereal and links of sausage into her trolley. As she made her way to the wines and spirits department we made our excuses and legged it!!

We don't ask forgiveness from the old lady, who we feel enjoyed her trip round the supermarket, but from the security guard and manager who both attempted to stop a surprisingly strong and determined pensioner as she ran from the shop with a trolley full of stolen goods.

Eddie, Peter, Neil, Richard.

Dear Simon,

My confession dates back to 1986 when I was a young sales representative working for a large grocery manufacturer – a household name, but one that I shan't give for reasons that will be revealed.

Calling regularly on supermarkets, I found myself one afternoon in the Shopping Giant Superstore in Oldham, Greater Manchester. I was ushered into the Manager's office and told he was a little tied up at present but would be with me in a few moments. Alone for a couple of minutes I gazed absent-mindedly around the office like you do, until my eyes came to rest upon a letter on his desk.

A quick read showed it to be from an irate customer, complaining that she'd brought some toffees from the store and discovered, upon getting home, that they were past their sell-by date. 'What are you going to do about it?' she asked. I did what anyone would do under the circumstances, and copied down the address at the top of the letter – just in case.

With it safely tucked away in my pocket, in came the manager. Soon business was done and I wandered off thinking little more about it. However, a couple of weeks later, alone in a hotel in Huddersfield with nothing much to do. I came upon the address once again.

The next move seemed obvious. Getting a pen and paper I put myself in the position of the manager and thought: 'Given a free hand, no store to worry about, how would he really like to reply to the complaint? With this in mind, I began: 'Dear Ratbag' and went on to explain that I couldn't care less about her comments because we had plenty of customers and that one less was okay as far as I was concerned.

The letter was posted the next morning and once again, I thought little more about it until, lying in bed several weeks later, I awoke to the radio news and an item that caught my attention. It said a customer of an Oldham supermarket had received a letter from the store after a complaint had been made; it was both rude and abusive and she was having none of it.

This all sounded strangely familiar and I thought – oo-er! – the jubilation that my little prank had met with such public success was mingled with the not unreasonable fear that if I was found out it would cost me my job. And the radio wasn't the only medium to pick up the story; the Mirror the Star, the Mail and Today all featured it, and I even became one of the few males ever to make Page 3 of the Sun.

But now, five years later, I feel it is time to confess and I hope that time has been sufficient to cover my tracks. I would like to apologize to the lady recipient of my letter and reveal that it was I, not the store, who sent it to you. Yes, all the handwriting tests on all those dozens of people were a waste of time – it was merely the warped sense of humour of a bored representative. But never mind, I heard about your appearance a few months later on a consumer affairs programme so I guess you got your mileage out of our little incident.

Above all, I would like to apologize to the store manager (I hope he's still with the company) who, according to the newspaper reports, suggested to the lady that she may well have written the letter herself. So, sorry to all concerned but – above all – Simon, am I forgiven?

Yours humbly (until the opportunity arises again!),
A. N. On.

Dear Crew,

I would like to recant the following tale with a warning:- Don't try this at home, in the studio, or elsewhere, it is dangerous.

In 1987 I was a postman in Peterborough, working there on the North Station, loading and unloading the mail-bags from the trains, with a tight-knit little team of other postmen. We often had a few laughs to alleviate the boredom of waiting for trains to arrive. The pattern was usually four minutes of frenetic humping (of bags) from the trains, lifting them onto 'haycarts' to be transported into the office, then waiting for the next train to be serviced.

We had a small hut where we could brew up, and cook light meals. Gaps between trains of 20 minutes or more were spent playing cards. The inspector, John, was okay for he could always take a joke. Another postman and I were renowned for japes and jokes, and between us we would always arrange to turn the regulator switch on Johns' gas lighter to either LOW , or flamethrower. After a few days of having his nasal hair removed or frustratingly trying to wear out his flint, he cottoned on to it. From that point on, the lighter never left his sight.

Until the Friday, that is. We were waiting a mail train at about 1800, and it was running sufficiently late to warrant a game of cards in the hut. Fifteen minutes into the game and we heard a familiar rumble. Necks craned and chairs scraped, and the late running train came into view. We shot out and serviced it, then split up to go to our appropriate points for the following trains.

On a Friday, it was usual to retire to the Great Northern, the railway hotel, and the Poachers' Bar, for a pint of the amber nectar. As everything was running smoothly, John ambled off for his pint, leaving us at work. It was barely 10 minutes later, when a steaming apparition came ambling down the platform at great speed, collared me and my mate and said I don't know, and don't care which of you two b———s it was, but Watch It In Future.

Not really having a clue what he was on about, it was with great merriment that we later learned the truth of the matter. John had gone to the bar, and settled on a stool, sipping his pint, when a blonde dream breezed in and sat down at the bar on another stool. She ordered her drink, and fetched a packet of cigarettes out of her handbag, placing one between her moist red lips, pouting slightly while she searched for her lighter. By all accounts she was a vision to behold (some of the lads from the office were in there at the time – much to John's embarrassment). Being a ladies' man, and a right smoothie, he slid from his stool and put on his best charms, saying something appropriate. Her eyelashes fluttered demurely as she accepted his offer of a light, bending low over his cupped hands. When the sheet of flame erupted, her carefully coiffured hair flew all over the place, her nose was filled with the stench of singed hair, and what eyebrows she had left after no doubt carefully plucking them, shrank from sight.

Gobsmacked and white, John stood there, no doubt time stood still, till a big cheer from 'the lads' must've startled him into action. He beat a hasty retreat, leaving his pint, and his cigarettes, and thus stormed off to approach us hard-at-work unfortunates.

To John, and the anonymous lady in question, I would like to say a big Sorry, and can think of no better argument to persuade both parties to pack up smoking.

Please may I be absolved?
Sam.

Dear St Simon,
After 20 years of torture, I feel now is the time to confess to a slight misdemeanour five friends and myself committed.

It was, if my memory serves me correctly, during the winter of 1970/71 and in the vicinity of Marks Gate, a delightful suburb of Chadwell Heath. As is the wont of bored teenagers, when snow lies thick on the ground, a chance of some harmless fun had fallen from the sky. As the main A12 trunk road ran close by Marks Gate it was always a great area of activity. With it being a main road buses ran along it quite frequently and had to slow down because of the Moby Dick roundabout (the Moby Dick being a pub on one corner). If you think back to the early seventies the old style London Transport buses had a stairwell at the back where the conductor used to stand. As the buses used to slow down for the roundabout six teenagers would leap up with a supply of pre-made snowballs and fire with unaccustomed accuracy.

After a number of direct hits we would retreat (like cowards) to a safe distance and listen to the dulcet tones of an irate bus conductor who, for some inexplicable reason, would raise questions as to our parentage.

With snowballs left over from the previous attack we started having a snowball fight. When one was thrown at me I ducked and it missed by inches. As I was out of ammunition I went to retrieve it only to find it had grown slightly after rolling in the snow. I called to the others that it would be a good idea to roll a big snowball. We set off with our small snowball and by the time we had finished rolling it was what can only be described as enormous.

The only question now was what to do with it. When we finished rolling the snowball we were just outside High View House, a 16-storey block of flats. The suggestion came that it would be fun to take it to the top and throw it out the window. This idea went down rather well with the rest of us so we pushed the snowball to the entrance and the lifts. The lift arrived but unfortunately there was not enough room for all five of us plus a big snowball, so the snowball, a friend and I went up in one lift and the other three went up in another.

Our problems started when half-way up the lift stopped, the doors opened and looking in was a dear old lady, whose expression changed from relief that the lift was working, to one of shock and horror at the sight of one boy squashed in the corner of the lift and another sat on a four-foot snowball. All I could say was 'Hello, if you hold on another one will be along in a minute'. The doors closed and we continued to the top of the building.

By this time, being in a warm lift, our snowball had melted slightly, flooding not only the floor of the lift but the lift shaft as well. We emerged from the lift on the 16th floor and met up again with the other three. The windows on all floors were of the slatted variety which just slid out from their sockets. We took out the first two and leant out. The coast was clear. We took out the remaining slats and manhandled the snowball that now resembled a three-foot round ice-cube onto the sill.

At this point we hesitated, should we or should we not. We should — and we did. After what seemed an eternity instead of the dull thud we expected there was a loud bang. In panic we ran for the lift, got in and pressed the button for the fourth floor. When we reached our destination we crept quietly down the last few flights of stairs. Surprisingly there was nobody about. We had a quick look to see how much glass was on the ground. I think our hearts disappeared into our underpants as we fled into the snow-filled night.

Simon, we do not beg forgiveness from the bus conductors, we do not beg forgiveness from the old lady who for all we know may have had a heart attack at the sight of two teenagers and a large snowball in the lift, but we do beg forgiveness from the poor unfortunate person who happened to park their almost new car just where a three-foot round ice-cube fell, causing what can only be described as a crater in the bonnet.

Please forgive us Simon and Rod, I know Dianne won't, as I and my friends would like to make a fresh start.

Yours faithfully,
Colin.

Dear Simon,

In 1981, when I was 19, I lived and worked in London, and got myself engaged to Ralph, who was an overseas buyer of sports equipment for a well-known chain of leisure outlets. In addition to being tall, bronzed, with a beautiful body and a black belt in karate – a real macho man – he could also provide me with frequent trips abroad when he had to go buying. So I had many weekends in Paris, the odd week in Spain and Italy, and even three weeks in Sydney, Australia.

Then came the big trip. He was picked to go to America for five months, travelling around, buying gear. I was all set to jack in my job and go with him, but he talked me out of this, pointing out that I would lose my chance of promotion, ruin my career – and, he emphasized, he saw my career as being as important as his – and besides, he would be too busy to spend much time with me. Being a little green, I agreed with him, and stayed behind in London.

Then a mutual friend, who had driven Ralph to the airport, told me that Ralph had taken A.N. Other to the States with him.

I was mildly annoyed, all the more so because I couldn't wreak the kind of revenge I wanted to. His house was locked up for the duration, heavily alarmed, and I didn't have a key, so no going round and calling the weather in New York and leaving the phone off the hook, or leaving the taps running.

Then I recalled that Mr Macho Ralph had one phobia – and I mean phobia – which reduced him to a quivering wreck. I went to the petshop, bought two breeding pairs of mice, dropped them through his letter box, and left them to get on with it. I sneaked round each night after dark to drop food through the door for the wee beasties.

Ralph, in the end, was away for seven months, during which time I got his 'Sorry, I've met someone else' letter.

Finally, the great day came when he came home. The same mutual friend who had driven to the airport, collected him. Ralph got to his house, de-activated the elaborate alarm system (which wasn't working any way, because the mice had chewed the wiring), opened the door, and stepped inside, with his arm round his new lady.

When he saw the evidence of the mice, he freaked. He was so terrified he wet himself. His new girlfriend was not impressed. Ralph had to call in Rentokil to get rid of the mice, but even then, he couldn't bear to stay in the flat because he knew the mice had been there, and he was forced to put the house on the market. It took ages to sell, as the neighbours – who had never liked Ralph – made sure potential buyers knew all about the rodent infestation. In the end, he had to drop the asking price by £2,500 to get the place sold.

After all these years, I have got to admit that I feel guilty . . . about the fate of the mice, who were after all the innocent victims in all of this, and who met such an untimely end. Do you think I can be forgiven?

Yours, penitently,
Kathy.

Dear Simon,
The more I think about this incident the more I realize I ought to seek forgiveness.

I don't know about you, but my main Saturday morning entertainment when I was aged 14 was to hang around in town. But Cambridge city centre in 1972 wasn't that exciting – it probably still isn't. So Geoff, Pete and myself decided to broaden our horizons, do something more constructive and give ourselves a greater challenge in life by hanging around in a bigger town. Th biggest, London.

I don't feel any guilt about travelling back and forth to London on a platform ticket, or even about fare dodging on the Underground. There's worse to come. We went to Kensington High Street and mooched around the shops until we discovered one called Biba which was more interesting than most. But we'd only been in there a few minutes before everyone was hustled out onto the pavement because of a bomb alert (nothing to do with us I hasten to add). Everyone hung around outside the shop and the police only kept us about 20 feet from the shop. We sat on the barrier at the edge of the pavement, eating crisps and waited for something to happen.

The police operation was being co-ordinated by a police sergeant. He was very impressive, tall, calm and brave with a medal ribbon on his

chest. He fearlessly searched the shop and reassured the worried staff outside. We'd been out on the pavement for a while and nothing had happened, but having finished my crisps, I blew up the bag and burst it. It certainly made a few people jump. Not least the big police sergeant, he threw himself face down on the pavement with his hands over his head, much to the amusement of all the people watching.

Fortunately I could run quite fast then and he stopped chasing me after a few hundred yards. If he'd caught me I probably wouldn't be here to ask your forgiveness.

Anyway, I regret humiliating such a dignified officer in front of all those people, so any chance of absolution?

Yours sincerely,
Rik.

Dear Simon,

I am asking forgiveness for something that happened in 1989 whilst I was in California. I had joined a Metaphysical church which was full of 'warm, friendly, genuine people' (aren't all Californians warm, friendly, genuine people??). I soon became 'one of the family', and was invited to attend the Rev. Ethel's healing and spiritual development circle. There I sat praying, meditating and talking with those 'warm, friendly, genuine people'. Then came the end of the session, which was dedicated to sending out healing prayers to friends and family. Rev. Ethel spoke the names of two unwell people Jill and Ken. Then to my utter surprise everyone began to sing 'Jill and Ken, Jill and Ken, Jill and Ken.' Little did they know they were singing those names to a well-known *Watch with Mother* tune.

Finally, it was my turn, the Rev. Ethel solemnly asked me, 'Peter . . . do you have anyone you would like to send out healing prayers to?' I couldn't resist it . . . with tears in my eyes, I uttered the names . . . 'Bill and Ben.'

I would like these 'warm friendly, genuine people' to forgive me for making them sing Bill and Ben, Bill and Ben, Bill and Ben. Of course I couldn't join in as I was in too much pain from trying to stop myself laughing and adding the words, 'Flowerpot Men' at the end of their little ditty. Am I forgiven?

Yours,
Peter.

Dear Father Simon,
Bless me, Father, for I have sinned. Several years ago when I was but a naive teenager, I was working in the local hospital pathology laboratory on a work experience scheme.

Being of an impressionable age, I was naturally carried away with enthusiasm for my job and was absolutely fascinated by the surrounding paraphernalia. I was particularly attracted to the gaudy yellow stickers used for identifying potentially hazardous waste materials (for example, Radioactive and Biohazard stickers). Therefore I could not resist the temptation to 'borrow' – steal – a quantity of the aforementioned labels for future use. On my way home I visited the local supermarket to pick up the week's provisions and, putting my hand in my pocket to retrieve my shopping list, instead I pulled out the wad of stickers.

Suddenly a fiendish and cunning plan sprang to my mind. Furtively, I made my way to the frozen food sections and, after checking that I was unobserved, I proceeded to attach the labels to a quantity of frozen chickens. I then casually strolled to the Checkout, leaving I know not what chaos behind.

So can I please be forgiven for the outbreak of vivid yellow warning labels saying 'BIOHAZARD, DANGER OF INFECTION' attached to the majority of the frozen poultry? I'm sure any resultant food scare was blown out of all proportion by the local press. I now see the error of my ways and promise faithfully never to repeat my actions.

Yours faithfully,
A repentant laboratory scientist.

3

The Green-Eyed Monster

Whoever it was who decided that it is possible to go green with envy, was clearly colour blind. Just a cursory glance at the next few pages will suggest alternative, more believable, colours. White with excruciating agony, and red with blind fury are two that come to mind.

Dear Simon,

Many years ago, when I was married to my ex, who was in the army at the time, he came home on leave for the weekend bringing the wife of an army pal whose marriage was going through a bad patch. He said she needed cheering up – Well I was only aged 18, and seriously stupid.

One evening, just before our evening meal was ready – he'd cooked a curry and I was doing the rice – it suddenly dawned on me with a dreadful clarity, that they were having an affair. I sat stunned for a moment or two, then calmly excused myself, left for the kitchen where I removed my underwear I'd been wearing all day, sewed up the legs and strained their share of the rice through them!

I don't want to be forgiven. I enjoyed that meal, and I've enjoyed the memory immensely on many occasions since. Furthermore I intend to go on enjoying it.

Have I won a car?

R.H.

Dear Simon,

I am writing to you in the hope that I may be able to shed some guilt. For I feel I ought to confess to something which started out as a wind-up and a joke, but finished up with someone being wound-up and broke.

Several years ago, I worked for a small kitchen sales business as an office-boy. I was 16 years old, with high hopes and great ambitions. I was never one to moan, and although I didn't get paid much, was quite happy with my lot.

I came into regular contact with the sales team, and got on fine with them all – that is, apart from Jeremy, who seemed to have it all. He had the gift of the gab, smart suits, a flashy car, his own pad and a stream of attractive girlfriends. Maybe it was jealousy, but whatever it was, I despised him, and despite his more-than-comfortable salary + commission + perks + anything else he could get his hands on, he also complained of not having enough money.

One day I was making the entire staff a cup of coffee, as all 16-year-old office juniors do, when in the next room, I heard him making a secret phone call on an external line. He was talking to his bank manager, trying to negotiate an overdraft and, by the sound of it, he wasn't having much luck. I thought no more of it until two days later, when Jeremy was out of the building, probably sliming round some poor unsuspecting customer in a bid to rip them off good and proper and increase his commission, and the bank manager phoned the office. He asked to speak to him. I said he wasn't available, and could I take a message. The manager merely asked me to tell Jeremy the answer was no.

He returned a while later, and because he couldn't park his BMW anywhere else, he casually threw my Honda 50 to one side. On entering, I quizzed him at length about this – I said 'What do you think . . .' and his reply was 'When you're a man you'll learn about priorities and respect.'

What a XXXX, I thought. Then I remembered the bank manager's message. I went downstairs into the coffee room, and made a phone call to the sales office upstairs. In my deepest, most disguised voice, I informed Jeremy that as one of the bank's best customers, I had decided to grant him an overdraft facility of £3000, interest free, with no time limit on repayments.

Obviously he was very pleased with this news, but subsequently became very ill, complaining of headaches, stomach aches, diarrhoea and just about every symptom he could think of. For four days he was off sick, throughout which the bank was constantly trying to get in touch with him. My boss suggested he would find him at home, but the bank manager had tried this, and found no sign of life.

Upon returning to the office the following week, Jeremy confided in me, telling tales of a trip to Amsterdam with his mate – the girls, the drinks, the wacky-baccy in the coffee-bars and the strip shows. He had obviously spent a fortune. The sales manager appeared promptly, and handed him an official document, 'Is this my Sick Pay certificate?' Jeremy greedily demanded. 'No. It's your P45. You're sacked!' came the reply.

That was the last I saw of him. However, I did hear that he had a County Court Summons issued against him, for fraudulent issuing of cheques on an account with no funds. I also heard that the flashy BMW was repossessed.

I feel as though an apology is probably due. All I can say is that I'm sorry, but if Jeremy is reading this, having managed to get back into a similar lifestyle, just remember, it's not just the oldies that you should respect.

Any chance of being forgiven?

Yours sincerely,
Robert.

Dear Father Simon,

I am deeply ashamed. I let my emotions run away with me and, well, things got a little out of hand.

It all happened on holiday in France. I went with a group of friends and met the most charming, attractive Englishman. Near the end of the second week, when I had begun to wonder why I had bothered to pay my share of the hotel room, I found out a terrible secret. This charming, attractive, sweet man, was married. His wife thought he was on a business trip somewhere in Milan. I was shocked and began to plot my revenge, because he was not going to get away with this.

The next day I told him I was going to ski with my friends for that day. As I normally met them for lunch he did not mind (if he only knew), and told me where he would be if I wanted him. I wanted him all right but not in the way he thought.

I went off and borrowed one of my friend's jackets, skis, ski pants and hat. I was disguised and ready. Now the charmer was not a very good skier. When I reached the top of the mountains I saw him. I skied down, picked the spot, just over a five-foot cliff. I raced down yelling at

him in french to get out of the way, clipped the back of his skis and sent him flying over the cliff. He was screaming 'I'm going to die, I'm going to die.' I left him rolling down the bank.

I also wrote his wife a note and sent it to his address with some incriminating evidence to show her husband was cheating on her, but what I want forgiveness for is this – that night I met him in the bar and he could not wait to tell me about this mad Frenchman who had tried to kill him earlier that day and how he had seen him again at the bottom of the lift and told him, what he thought of him.

So, it is forgiveness, Father Simon, that I want for landing the Frenchman (who happened to be a professional skier) out of the ski season and into hospital with a broken finger and six stitches after a nasty accident with a ski pole being wrapped around his head.

Am I forgiven for hurting this innocent bystander?

The man and his wife are now divorced and I got a thank you note from his wife. (She did not know who I was.)

Thank you,
Louise.

Dear Simon,

Some 25 or so years ago, I was asked to assist at a church Jumble Sale and take the surplus clothing to a local Rag and Bone Merchant who would give us a good price for the rags. Being an obliging soul, I promised to accomplish the task the following day in my lunch hour. Along with two colleagues Andy and Alan, who worked in the same office, we collected the jumble and, whilst loading it into my car, it was noticed that it included intimate items of ladies underwear – so we removed a number of bras from the bundle before delivering the rest of the clothes to the Ragman.

We then returned to work, but before entering the office we toured the car park and to our delight found three cars unlocked and in each we placed one of the said items. The three bras we chose were in differing styles – one big enough to cover a centurion tank, another extremely grubby and the third a saucy little black number.

Next day word started to spread around the office about mysterious discoveries in staff cars. Apparently Mick made no more of finding the tank cover than to wave the same at three girls from the typing pool as they left the office shouting, 'Does this belong to any of you?'

Gerald, a secretive fellow, took some time to admit he had even found the grubby bra and apparently had gone to great lengths to hide the article. The real problem arose with Graham, the recipient of the saucy bra. His fiancee worked in the same office and after work he took her and two other female colleagues home. One of the girls found the bra on the back seat and discreetly asked Graham's betrothed how she had come to leave it there. It seems all Graham's attempts to laugh off the incident as some sort of practical joke were to no avail and the journeys the following week were particularly unpleasant for him.

I think we perpetrators were always suspected by the three blokes, but it is from the ladies involved we seek forgiveness.

Paul.

P.S. The saucy black bra eventually found its way into the office where it became a feature of office life for some years, turning up in desks, filing cabinets and other places where the embarrassment of others could be achieved. It was last seen in a leaving present.

Dear Simon,

Many years ago, in the late 70s, I was a housewife looking after young children. I had a husband who did not take kindly or readily to married life – his idea and mine of what a marriage should be like differed immensely. I thought husbands remained faithful to their wives, but he seemed to disagree.

There I was struggling to be a good Mum and wife with what I found to be an errant husband. He would dress up for the evening, go out, and not return until either the early hours or the following day.

Simon, in those days I was such an innocent wife, believing and gullible. I believed him when he said he slept on a mate's settee as he'd had too much to drink. Finally I realized I was kidding myself and that my husband was using and abusing my good and innocent nature.

I got proof when one of his girlfriends – I found out he had two at that time – knocked on my door for 'her boyfriend', my husband. That was it – I thought – he's had it. Like Baldrick I had a cunning plan.

My husband liked spicy foods, onions, curry, garlic, spices and chilli peppers, so I cooked these quite often. Years earlier I had discovered that small chilli peppers contain big power. If your nose or face itches while you are chopping the peppers and you inadvertently scratch them with hands containing some of the chilli juices the effect is an excruciating, burning and throbbing pain.

So I bought some strong chillies, chopped them in half and, making sure my hubby was out, I took all his clean underwear and rubbed the crotch of each pair of pants he possessed with chillies.

It's worth remembering that in the late 70s the fashion was bright coloured hipster briefs which hugged all the figure tightly. So when the chillies were rubbed vigorously and squashed into the garment I made sure all evidence of peppers was removed, then carefully folded and put away his nether garments. And I waited.

The next night, he bathed and dressed in clean clothes – including the doctored articles – ready to go out. Nothing appeared amiss, and so off he went.

In the days following my poor hubby complained of painful and burning sensations in his tender regions – a hot throbbing to be precise. I played very innocent, explaining I hadn't changed the washing powder so it couldn't be that. I suggested perhaps he hadn't cleaned all the Ajax powder from the bath when he had wiped it down, but he didn't seem to think it was that.

I eventually washed all his underwear, feeling I had wreaked my revenge. To this day I don't know if he sought medical treatment, but I bet the thought crossed his mind, nor do I know what happened to his girlfriend.

So Simon, I wish to be forgiven. I'm older and much wiser now and well divorced. I know his new wife will have all the same problems as I had so I bear her no ill will. I do not want to be forgiven for causing him indescribable pain and the thought that he had probably acquired some strange and unwanted disease.

But I do ask forgiveness of the girlfriends on that occasion. I'm sure they must have shared in some of his sufferings and have been accused of various misdemeanours. I know they did not know he was married and so were as gullible as I. Please may I be forgiven?

You may now uncross your legs.

Joy.

Dear Simon,

It's time for me to confess to something a friend of mine – who I shall call Trevor – and I did five years ago.

We had a friend called Fred, who was a terribly trendy advertising executive with a large advertising agency. Trevor and I both worked in the same industry, but for a much smaller agency, and we got rather sick of hearing Fred constantly drone on about how much money he earned, what house he was able to afford, the exclusive restaurants he frequented, the absolute necessity of his mobile phone, and other such materialistic drivel. (Not, of course, that we weren't materialistic – we just couldn't afford what he could and so we affected a 'phooey, who needs all that capitalistic rubbish' attitude, borne out of nothing more highflown than sheer envy.)

Fred was particularly fond of his car – a BMW 320i, complete with personalized numberplate – and one day, Trevor and I were complaining about the amount of car tax we had to pay on our company cars, which were nothing like as posh as Fred's. This caused Fred to laugh in a particularly snide way, and say wasn't it funny, he was only taxed £XX per year, and yet his car was worth far more than ours.

That was it. We were fed up with being his proletariat friends. So, it was funny that he paid far less than us wasn't it? We'd show him. We decided to sit down and compose a short letter, supposedly from a colleague of Fred's saying: 'Dear Inland Revenue, I have worked for XXX agency for the past four years, and I have been informed by my colleague, Fred Kelly, that my car tax is inaccurate. I pay £XX per year for a BMW 320i, but he says I should only pay £XX, just as he does. Can this be true? Yours etc . . .'

Nothing happened for absolutely ages, the bailiffs didn't arrive at Fred's bijou cottage to repossess everything to compensate for years of unpaid car tax – nothing. We forgot all about it until one day, about 12 months later, Fred came storming into the wine bar we frequented, ranting on about those beggers at the Tax Office that had stung him for an absolute fortune in unpaid car tax. We sniggered into our white wine and sodas (typical advertising drink at the time, although I preferred a gin and tonic and Trevor liked a pint of bitter) and commiserated with Fred. He was going to have to sell his personalized numberplate to help pay for it apparently, and it looked as though the planned holiday in Barbados we'd heard so much about was now off.

I had to go to the ladies toilets to laugh out of the window – much to the surprise of a couple of late-night shoppers passing underneath – compose myself and then return to Fred. He was absolutely fuming and not about to let the subject drop. 'Some miserable little sneak's shopped me,' he ranted, 'and I bet I know who,' he added. Trevor and I immediately discovered we had pressing appointments elsewhere and left him to cry into his soda water (he was now on an economy drive).

Worse was to follow. Fred became convinced his new junior assistant had shopped him to the Inland Revenue and made the poor girl's life a misery to such an extent that after two months, she left.

Time has now passed, Trevor and I both left the advertising industry to resume a life of normality, and I am only writing this because last week we heard that Fred was made redundant. Now instead of having his go-faster car and a mobile phone, he catches the bus and is saving up for a Phonecard. Tee hee.

We're not actually that bothered about receiving Fred's forgiveness, but Trevor and I would like to apologize to Tanya, Fred's assistant, whose life he made a misery because he blamed her for our wrong doings. Tanya, we're sorry. Do you forgive us?

Yours,
Lucy.

Dear Simon,

Despite the following incident dating back nearly 10 years I am afraid this will have to be an Anon confession.

I was a student at Nottingham University and stayed in a mixed (male and female) hall of residence. There was a girl called Jane who I (and half of the other male inmates) fancied like mad, but despite all my efforts of holding doors open, accidentally bumping into her, and so on, she never really acknowledged my existence.

I persevered and saw my big chance coming at the end-of-term dinner dance when, due to blackmail, corruption and extortion, I managed to get myself not just on her table but sitting next to her. I tried everything to start up a conversation with Jane but all my advances were rebuffed. Instead she threw all her attentions at the curly-haired football-type sitting opposite and kept taking posey type photographs of him with a small camera she had with her.

Towards the end of the meal Jane excused herself and left to powder her nose. It was then I noticed she had left her camera on my side of the table. I can remember looking at it and thinking she had taken so many photos of Kevin Keegan I'm surprised she hasn't asked him to pose naked when an idea suddenly came into my warped and twisted mind. Inconspicuously I picked up her camera, excused myself, and skulked out of the dining room . . . and straight into the men's toilets which was at full capacity. I went up to the nearest person, held Jane's camera above his head pointing at his feet, and pressed the button. Before the poor chap could turn around to see what was going on I was back in the dining room with Jane's camera sitting where I had found it.

I would like to ask for forgiveness not only from Jane and the poor bloke innocently relieving himself in the proper place, but also from Jane's mum. As this was the end-of-term dinner dance Jane had got the film developed when she had returned home for the vacation and was so keen to show Mummy pictures of her new boy friend she hadn't screened them first.

Am I forgiven?

Anon.

4

The British Abroad . . . and at Home

Your parents were right. 'Just because you're on holiday, it doesn't mean that all codes of civilized behaviour, learnt over the brief history of human development, can be jettisoned for your two week convenience.' Well, my parents talk like that anyway.

Essential holiday reading.

Dear Simon,
Although this isn't my own confession it's one I think that you'd find amusing.

The incident happened a couple of years ago on a caravan site in Norfolk. Four lads were on holiday having fun and as lads do – creating a lot of noise and havoc, wild parties, and so on. The family in the next caravan to theirs got a bit fed up with all the noise, and complained to the site owner. The lads were thrown off the site and the family then enjoyed a peaceful few days.

Until one night, when they came back after a night out to find the caravan door wide open. They rushed inside expecting to find it burgled but everything was in its place and nothing was missing. So they thought they had left the door unlocked and didn't think any more about it. They finished their holiday in peace and tranquillity and went home fully relaxed.

A couple of weeks later they got their photos back from being developed, and upon looking through them they found one they didn't remember taking. It had three of the lads mooning to the camera – which isn't so bad – but whilst doing the mooning they had inserted the family toothbrushes in a very unusual place. Let's say they weren't cleaning their teeth with them.

The family immediately dumped the toothbrushes, as they had been using the 'soiled' toothbrushes since their holiday. Although they did buy new ones, apparently cleaning their teeth has never been the same since.

Michelle.

Dear Simon & Co,

Whilst in Greece on holiday with my best mate, we found ourselves drinking at a local tavern. We spotted two lovely-looking young ladies sitting outside in the warm sun, and bravely decided to go chat them up.

My mate, who is tall, dark and handsome, obviously had no problem, but I, being short, pale, ugly and balding, had no chance. We chatted for a while, well they did, but my mate completely left me out, feeling like an idiot. He then arranged to meet both the girls later in the evening. He even had them to call for him at his hotel room at 7 pm!

I went back to my room, a little despondent to say the least, wondering what to do with my night. I suddenly had an awful, evil and nasty thought. I ran downstairs and out into the little village to find a chemist. I eventually found a shop which sold toiletries etc. I asked the old lady for a sachet of hair removing cream for my 'wife', and left with a packet, grinning to myself.

I rushed up to my mate's room and let myself in; then carefully squeezed the contents into his shampoo bottle which was almost

empty, as he washes his hair twice a day! I then left his room, already feeling guilty. He later returned and, as every other night and morning, washed his hair and showered.

He had rubbed the whole bottle of shampoo-cum-hair remover, all over himself, and had tufts of hair coming away as he dried himself. He shouted from his door for me to come quickly, I ran over, and he was hysterical!

Clumps of hair had come away from his scalp, his eyebrows were thinner, plus most of the hair on his arms was gone, as he'd obviously rubbed shampoo 'all over' if you know what I mean. He began crying, and could not believe what was happening. I felt really bad for what I had done. He thought he'd caught a social disease or had eaten the foreign food and it hadn't agreed with him.

He spent the rest of the holiday on his balcony, I got to take the two girls out, as he was 'ill in bed', I had a wonderful evening, with my mate back at the hotel!

After writing this down, I realize that I cannot be forgiven, or can I?

Yours faithfully,
Andy.

P.S. His hair has fully grown back now.

Dear Father Simon,

I am writing to you in the hope that you will grant me absolution for the terrible sin that I committed, and grant me serenity from my guilt!

Last July I went to stay with my friend Howard at his flat in Bournemouth for a few days. On the last day of my stay I awoke early and after waving Howard off to work, I decided to take a bath. I went into the bathroom, ran the bath, and feeling slightly chilly, I decided to close the 'tilt and turn'-style window before removing my dressing gown. The window had been wide open all night, as the day before had been very hot and humid.

On closing the window, I was amazed to see at least a bucketful of water fall out of the window down into the garden below. On closer inspection I discovered the glass was inset into the frame which protruded by about three inches. It had obviously rained in the night and the water collected, but it was invisible to the eye until the window was closed. I thought no more about it and got in the bath.

Just as I had finished my ablutions, I heard the front door bell ringing furiously. I went to the intercom to inquire who it was, to be told 'Good morning madam, this is the Dorset Constabulary. Open up in the name of the law!' I got the shock of my life, immediately suspecting Howard to have done something very wrong (yes I know he's my friend but even so . . .). I pulled on my dressing gown (even though I was still wringing wet), wrapped my newly washed hair in a towel and went down to the front door.

On opening the door I was thrust back against the wall, door still in my hand, by about 20 uniformed officers and at least five plainclothes officers who, on discovering I was not staying with Howard's next door neighbour, then proceeded to try and demolish the neighbour's front door, in an effort to obtain entry. By now, I was very worried and crept back to Howard's flat where I hid in the lounge and watched and listened to the goings on outside. Three officers were digging up the garden looking for I know not what, others were patrolling the front of the flats and the road outside, whilst goodness knows how many were attempting to get at poor unfortunate Simon, Howard's next door neighbour. After some 45 minutes Simon emerged, was arrested in the front garden, put into a police car, with much shouting and swearing, and I distinctly heard him cry out, 'That was not me'.

That night when Howard came home from work, I told him what had happened, and he went next door to see Simon. We still don't know the real reason why the police came for Simon in the first place, but it appears that during the latter part of the morning in question they tried to book Simon for assaulting an officer, as he allegedly threw a bucket of water over them as they stood at the door awaiting to be let in . . .

I would like to sincerely apologise to Simon, the five wet plainclothes detectives I unfortunately drenched that morning, and also to Simon, whom to this day isn't sure whether I deliberately got him into trouble or not!

Please Father Simon absolve me of my sin and plead for my forgiveness from Father Rod and Mother Dianne!

Yours sincerely,
Susan.

Dear Simon,

My little story takes place in France in 1988. I was at secondary school at the time and was on one of those notorious French exchanges. We had exchanged with a school in a town about 50 km south of Paris and, being so close to Paris, we went on a day trip there. There must have been about 40 of us on the exchange plus four members of staff and a somewhat grumpy coach driver.

On our visit to Paris we were given some time to roam around on our own. While we were doing this my friend Pete managed to find a shop that sold loads of army stuff including small aerosols of 'Crowd Control Gas', alias 'Tear Gas'. Well, my friend Pete, being a good English schoolboy, bought a can.

When we got back on the coach and were winding our way along one of the dual carriageways on our way to have lunch at some park or other, Pete decided to show me what he'd bought. I thought it would be a bit of fun to let just a bit of it off. So I did. Now Tear Gas can be pretty devastating stuff when used on streets full of rioters like you see on the news so I think that if you multiplied its effect by 10 you'd understand what it did to a coachload of schoolkids. First of all you get a funny taste in your mouth, then the taste turns sour, then your eyes water, then your stomach starts to retch, then you feel dizzy, then you really want to vomit. This goes on for quite a time.

Anyway, having stopped the coach and let 40 rather green-looking kids evacuate onto the central reservation, Mrs Watkins (head of French) started looking for the guilty party. It was pretty soon narrowed down to me and Pete. I really am sorry Pete for what happened next. I really am sorry that I protested my innocence and left you to get your ear pierced by Mrs Watkins nails. I really am sorry you were condemned for the rest of the trip. I'm sorry it was you who never saw eye-to-eye with Mrs Watkins again. But, I have to say, it couldn't have happened to a nicer chap.

Am I forgiven?

By the way, Pete and I are still great chums and I hope that in raking up the past I won't change that!

Yours faithfully,
James of Tilford.

Dear Simon & Crew,

In August 1971 we went on our family holiday. This particular year it was to Littlehampton, I was aged 13 and my sister was 16. Our parents thought we were old enough to behave, and booked us in a room on our own.

When we arrived at the Guest House ours was the attic room at the top of the house. While unpacking we wondered what the whooshing noise was coming from a cupboard in the corner. When we opened it we found the cistern from the toilet on the floor below. There was a piece of string attached to the handle which went through a hole in the floor to be pulled to flush the toilet.

Our parents were in a room on the floor below and, sitting on the top of the stairs, we could see their bedroom door. We watched our dad leave the room heading out of sight for the toilet. We heard the toilet door close, then a few minutes later heard the cistern flushing in our bedroom cupboard.

We decided we would wait until the next day to put our plan into action. As we sat at the top of the stairs our dad came out of the bedroom, disappeared out of sight, and, when we heard the toilet door, we ran into the bedroom giving time to undo trouser, pull down, sit on seat . . . then we flushed the toilet from upstairs, then rolled around laughing on the bed.

When we went down to breakfast with our parents, dad said, 'You'll never guess what happened this morning' (my sister and I held our laughter), 'I went to go to the toilet when this woman beat me to it, so I waited outside. When she came out she said 'watch that toilet, it has a mind of it's own. It flushed while I was sitting on it.'

Please say sorry to the poor woman with the wet bottom, and forgive me, my sister and my dad, for when we told him we had done it he laughed too.

Yours hopefully,
Linda.

Dear Simon,

My shameful story goes back to the summer of '82 and the island of Ibiza. On holiday with my friends, life was wonderful, the weather glorious, in fact it was FUN FUN FUN !

One night in one of the copious bars that adorn San Antonio we met a group of girls from Liverpool. They were young, suntanned, happy, and drunk. We were young, suntanned, happy and even drunker. After a while they invited several of us back to their apartments for a party and, loaded with booze, we staggered off to continue our revels.

I was getting on very well with one particular young lady until she asked me what I did for a living. Not wishing to admit that in those days I was a boring bank clerk, I told her I was a hairdresser.

You guessed it! Egged on by my mischievous mates I offered to cut her hair. This trusting young soul was agreeable and after dousing her hair rather professionally and draping a towel around her shoulders I set to work with a pair of nail scissors. I went beserk hacking away in an attempt to produce what I fondly considered as a Bananarama hairstyle.

Well, the girl seemed quite satisfied in her somewhat inebriated state and the party ended after a while. With the onset of the cold (well, bloody hot actually) light of day I realized what I had done. For the rest of the holiday I never went near that particular bar or apartment block, but then again I don't suppose she left her room either. I have been told by my wife and various female friends that I could never be forgiven. Please can you put me out of my misery and grant me absolution?

As you can appreciate, this letter must remain anonymous not because of the nature of my job but because of the fear of attacks by the girls in the office showing feminine solidarity with their coiffured colleague.

Yours sincerely,
Mr Midnight.

Dear Simon,

It all happened about 20 years ago when my big sister was away in Austria on an exchange visit. As a measure of consolation to make up for the fact that she was away for a whole month in foreign climes, my parents agreed to take my best mate of the time, John, and I away on a 'glamorous' week's holiday in a caravan at sunny Morecambe.

We arrived at the site in late afternoon. Within 10 minutes John and I had completely explored the area and realized its potential for two rowdy 11-year-olds – to wit, not a lot! There was a games room with three old-fashioned slot machines and an extremely ancient table tennis table – but no bats or balls. How were we to amuse ourselves on this bleak and unpromising site for a whole week?

We pondered this problem as we walked the half-mile to the toilet block that evening to complete our ablutions. This walk involved passing the edge of a field which contained a very scruffy-looking goat, which provided milk and cheese for the farm next door to the site to sell to tourists. As we walked along, we leant on this goat's wall to decide what to do. She was very friendly and accustomed to people from the caravan site coming up to her and giving her all sorts of tasty tit-bits to supplement the somewhat boring diet of grass provided by her habitat. So, as John and I leant on her wall, up she came nagging for the goodies she was sure we had brought for her.

Did we have any food for her? No, we didn't, but then we found something very interesting; it became apparent that our goaty pal liked the taste of the soap John and I were carrying to have the wash that young boys are, of course, always so keen to have. Having made this discovery, it was then a simple step to decide we could probably manage to get through the entire week without washing, and this we determined to do.

So, every morning and evening for the whole week, we would religiously set off for the toilet block, dissuading my parents from accompanying us, feed the soap to the goat and avoid the necessity for putting soap and water anywhere near our increasingly revolting bodies. Now, in her defence, it must be said that my mum became increasingly suspicious as we got smellier and smellier throughout the week.

'Are you two actually washing?', she would ask.

'Of course we are, Mum,' I would reply, 'Look how much soap we've used.'

She may not have been entirely convinced, but could prove nothing. So now, please can I confess to both my mum and John's mum that they were both right – we didn't wash at all.

But there is also another person to whom I need apologize – the farmer who owned the goat. The goat remained perfectly healthy (it's not a 'dead animal' confession) but the farmer could not understand why, after about four days of John and I feeding his prize milker, loads of people suddenly started complaining of a soapy taste in the goat's milk they were buying from the farm. He then went on a purge of his dairy to find out which part of his equipment was not being rinsed properly and thereby passing a lovely suds-like quality to his much-prized milk.

I feel safe in telling him now that it wasn't his dairy, but the peculiar diet his goat received for that week. I could also try to say it wasn't our fault but the goat's for nicking my soap in the first place – but I don't suppose I can get away with that.

As a postscript, having now experimented with not washing in this charmless way, I perfected it a couple of years later when I went on a long school trip to Austria. Then I succeeded in avoiding the attentions of the accompanying staff and managed to spend the whole four weeks without washing or changing my clothes!

My Mum knows about that one, though – she spotted it straight away (and smelt it too!).

Yours sincerely,
Graeme.

Dear Fr Simon,

I write but without the consent on behalf of seven friends of mine and of course myself, for absolution for a sin most foul.

Whilst in the Sixth Form the said number of friends and I went to stay in a caravan on the outskirts of Skegness for a week's holiday. One night, having frequented the majority of bars and indeed some of the off-licences, we made our way back to our temporary home in a rather loud and well-oiled way. On reaching the campsite the son of the caravan's owners pleaded for us to quieten down, as the other residents would undoubtedly complain to his father when he came to pick us up on the Saturday morning. Far from doing as requested we became louder and louder, so by the time we got into the caravan our mate was understandably worried.

Having tired of his constant attempts to shut us up, we all got dressed again and said we were going for a walk. Eight of us descended once more onto the now deserted streets of Skegness. We walked for some time before we turned to come home, but as we walked we didn't realize temptation was just around the corner. Down a dark lane, hidden amongst the back streets, we found a field. In it was a tent, and in the tent was a light; so bright that it silhouetted everything within. As we passed by, a figure pushed himself up from the ground and positioned himself to do press ups. These were the worst press ups that we had ever seen as if he kept his back straight and his arms locked.

Silence descended upon us. We knew we should leave but nobody was prepared to make the first move. Eventually almost as one we did move – not down the lane, but rather onto the three-foot-high wall that surrounded the field. There we sat, muffling our giggles, knowing what we were about to do. Eventually the athlete stood to a half-crouch and switched off the lamp. This was our cue. At the top of the sixth form decibel range, we shouted, clapped and applauded his efforts, knowing full well that the couple inside the tent could hear us loud and clear. We left the field, in stitches of laughter, wondering what the faces of the intimate couple looked like now they had been embarrassed beyond belief.

The rest, as they say, is history. We went back to the caravan, home the following Saturday and now most of the eight hold down good jobs, the other being in full-time education. On behalf of the eight of us I beg that the couple whose night we ruined will forgive us and that you Father Simon will forgive a very childish prank and not look upon us too harshly.

Yours reformingly,
Michael.

P.S. By way of reconciliation, we never returned to that camp site as a group of eight. The caravan we stayed in was a six-berth one and, believe me, after about the third day the smell of socks was overpowering. If you would take this into consideration when passing judgment it would be a weight off our minds.

Forgive us Father Simon for we have sinned.

The dastardly deed occurred during a college Duke of Edinburgh trip to the French and Swiss Alps during July of last year. The culprits Chris, Lucy, Matthew and myself, (these are false names to protect our identity), were seen as heroes when we were the only group of three, to complete a gruelling 60 km hike in the scorching heat up and down the Alps.

The group leaders were in awe of us as we completed the scheduled five day romp in just four days. The hike was strictly self-sufficient, surviving purely on supplies taken from the base camp in Les Contamines. We completed the romp in Trieste, Switzerland, to a rapturous heroes' welcome from the other groups and group leaders. It was smoochies all round as they helped us off with our 50 lb packs.

However, unbeknown to them, we cheated. At lunchtime on the fourth and final day we were near exhaustion and had used up our rations when we came upon a mountain top restaurant. Like an oasis in a desert, but still a cardinal sin to all hardened D of E'ers. We cared not for the rules and were soon tucking in to heaps of spaghetti and pizzas with gusto, which were paid for with most of our 'dire emergency' money.

Heartened by our banquet we marched on to our last few kilometres or so and one of our biggest obstacles: a 3000-ft climb over a mountain. The thought of struggling over this in 35°C soon doused our spirits, until we caught sight of the cable car peacefully winding its way up the mountain. We decided that as we had already cheated we might as well do it again and so spent the last of our money on the cable car. During our ride we felt a deep sense of guilt which must have lasted three or four seconds. When we reached the top, we had just an easy stroll down the mountain to our welcoming party.

We have since received our awards but we know that we don't really deserve them. To this day we are still heralded as an example to new recruits to the scheme at college for our determination and grit.

Signed,
Simon & Chris (co-writer/confessor).

5

Maniacs Behind the Wheel?

If you are a truly righteous person, you may be glowing by now, all over your smug angelic face. Your youth was blameless, your self-control is legendary, you've never been jealous of any one or thing, and your holidays are spent in monasteries.

Well, prepare to be penitent, for there is a machine to turn Mother Teresa into Ronnie Biggs with a BCCI bank account. Ladies and Gentlemen, the fiendish, demonic, soul destroyer known as . . . the automobile . . . .

Dear Simon,

I would like to confess to an incident that occurred about five years ago and has given me one or two sleepless nights since.

I was travelling on the Dumbarton to Helensburgh road, beside the picturesque River Clyde, on a typically winding road. The vehicles in front of me were travelling at a rather slow pace and, as usual, I was late for an important appointment. I was reasonably familiar with the road, and was continually pulling out, trying to find the opportunity to overtake the slow-moving traffic.

After getting more and more irate I finally decided to go for it, accelerated and pulled out to overtake on one of the few straight parts of the road, at the same time venting my anger and frustration at the drivers and their occupants of sounding my horn and pointing to my two fingers in a Harvey Smith-style towards them.

After making reasonable progress, passing some of the slow-moving vehicles, I was now in a position to see the front car, and beyond it the gap in the road. But to my horror, I realized the leading car was a hearse, on its way to the local crematorium. I then braked and, rather sheepishly slipped back, pulling in behind the mourning relatives.

I have since moved away from the area, but still would welcome forgiveness. Am I forgiven?

Yours sincerely,
Brian.

Dear Simon,

I've decided to write to you about something that happened 10 or 12 years ago. My dad had his own wholesale toy business, supplying beach balls, teddy bears, buckets and spades, and so on to resorts on the east and west coasts.

One Sunday at about 7 am there was a first delivery to Cromer, where there is a very steep slipway down to the beach. Half way down where fishing boats were launched, there was a little seaside shop. There was quite a bit of stuff to deliver, so dad decided it was best to reverse down the slipway to it. I was driving, as he jumped out to guide me down. As he was waving me back, doing the 'come on' and 'left hand down' bit, he recognized someone he knew up on the main raod and started to wave at him. I looked up the road to see who it was waving back at my dad, and just then I felt a slight 'bump' from the back of the truck. I checked both mirrors and stuck my head out of the window, but, my dad had vanished.

I jammed on the handbrake and jumped out of the cab, thinking I might just have done something my mother would not forgive me for. I ran back to the truck and saw I had bumped into a mobile ice cream kiosk, which had been propped up on bricks at one end to make it level on the steep cobbled slope. I say had been propped, as now it was slowly rolling down the slipway with my dad hanging on to the jockey wheel trying to stop it.

I tried to grab hold of my dad, but tripped over the bike chained to the kiosk (for safe keeping) which was being dragged down the slipway, now a little quicker. It was then that I became aware of the loud barking noise coming from inside the kiosk, which was rolling along quite quickly with my dad running behind still trying to stop it.

I just stood and watched, tears gathering in my eyes, helpless . . . with laughter. The kiosk, containing a dog, dragging a bike and my dad down the slipway, in just a few yards, had picked up quite a bit of speed. It made quite a splash when it hit the water at the bottom of the slipway.

After all the noise of this charade it suddenly went very quiet (apart from the berserk dog inside the kiosk!). My dad stood up to his bruised and scraped knees in the sea and looked around then at me, I looked around, then at him. There was no one else about. Without a word spoken we both ran back to the truck, got in and drove off.

The following week there was an article in the local rag about vandals smashing up the seafront, the ice cream salesman went 'bust' because the kiosk fell apart after it was rescued at low tide. The bike got a bit mangled, the shop lost its delivery and one of its main suppliers – my dad – never returned, the dog survived although lived in mortal fear of water and enclosed spaces.

To you all I am very sorry indeed, but it was half my dad's fault. I now live on the east coast and one of my sisters-in-law lives in Cromer.

I don't care if you forgive me, but it teaches my dad a lesson not to throw away my scalextric set. I am 34 years old.

Jasper.

Dear Father Simon,

In late 1988 my next door neighbour and rival James, and I both celebrated our seventeenth birthdays and immediately took to our parents' cars. We both jumped at each and every chance to practise driving.

In fact, the driving became almost an obsession between us, and it soon became a race to see who would pass first. James and I received our test dates at the same time, but mine was an hour earlier. However, a week before my test, I received a letter telling me it had been cancelled as I had requested. Surely there was some mistake. I checked with the test centre and they assured me there was no error. Whoever had cancelled my test had known when it was and also my personal code. It could only be James.

I decided to get my own back on him, in the best possible way – during the test itself. On the morning of the test, I woke early, crept outside and let his front tyres down (not completely, but enough to make steering difficult). However, I didn't realize it would cause him to crash the car. Believe it or not, he failed. There was £350 damage to the right wing, the bonnet and the milkfloat it hit.

James' second test was two days before my first. Again, I left the house early and this time waited behind a parked van with a football. As he came down the road, I rolled the ball in front of the car and saw him swerve to avoid it, before coming to a halt with his front wheels sitting on the kerb. He told me afterwards he'd failed on his emergency stop.

The day of my test came. After starting off well, things went horribly wrong on the emergency stop. However, I knew I had to carry on regardless. As I drove down a quiet road, a football shot out in front of the car, so I hit the footbrake and clutch and did another emergency stop – but perfectly this time.

At the end of the test the examiner turned to me and told me that, to my surprise I had passed. He told me that although I had failed my original emergency stop, when it had come to the real thing I had passed with flying colours. This did not go down at all well with James.

Even though I had passed, I thought it was necessary to wreak further revenge on him for his attempt at making me fail.

The night before his third test I managed to persuade a school friend to lend me his motor scooter for the following day. James was driving down a one-way street when I overtook him, and I then drove as slowly as I could in front of him. I managed to keep him below 20 miles an hour for almost five minutes before he overtook and it wasn't until two days later that I found out he had been failed for indecision on overtaking.

The pressure was really on James now, and it was costing him a fortune. I knew I no longer had to sabotage his tests – he'd lost his nerve. He eventually passed on the sixth attempt!

Well, Simon, I'd like to apologize to James who now lives in Bromley, and since I've now also moved house I know he'll never find me!

Yours cunningly,
Mark.

Dear Simon Mayo,

My tale unfolds during the Summer of 1980 when, being in the Navy, I was based and living in Gosport with my wife and two young children.

We decided, on a hot, sunny Saturday, to take advantage of the sea front at Southsea. So we packed up and drove there early in the morning. Now, the front at Southsea is a very popular parking area, with cars sitting in a herring-bone pattern, their bonnets pointing on to the seafront. After a very enjoyable day on the beach, we returned to the car to find that we were sandwiched between a very rusty Morris 1300, and a large camper-type van.

In the back of the camper, four pensioners were enjoying a picnic tea and were totally oblivious to the fact that each time I reversed out of my space, the boot of my car was nearly being hit by passing cars. My vision was restricted because of the size of the camper.

Then, a member of the tea party realized my predicament and held up his hand in the air in the manner of a traffic warden. He was telling me to wait, as the way was busy. His hand then waved in a 'come on' motion. So I promptly went into reverse, swung my steering wheel round and reversed out bringing the entire wing of the rust bucket on the other side, with me.

The 'Ooohs' on the faces of the pensioners will stay with me until my dying day, but their looks of concern were soon replaced, as I held up a pen and a piece of paper, pointing to the wingless car's windscreen. Yes, I was about to do the decent thing and restore their faith in the young. Well, I can only assume that the little red gremlin of insurance claims sat on my shoulder as I wrote: 'To whom it may concern. The people in the camper next to me think I'm leaving my name and address. I'm not am I?'

Having related this sordid tale, I feel a little absolved and can face my two children, Emma and Alan, with my head held high.

Mr X.

Dear Simon,

When I was younger a friend and I made a guy (as in Guy Fawkes and all that). Now, this guy was quite (for 'quite' read 'very') realistic. We'd been walking around our local town and collected a bit of dosh.

Unfortunately, we were bored. This led us to seek a way of relieving the said condition. As we were pondering, a single-decker bus rounded a corner heading towards us. We responded simultaneously. We took the guy and concealed ourselves behind a bush. As the bus drew level with us we hurled it at its windscreen!

What an actor – he spread his arms wide, face flat against the screen and, no doubt, showing a face of terror to the driver. His face was a picture – complete horror and panic. The bus swerved and slowed, with screeching tyres and passengers thrown everywhere.

The mortified driver, obviously in shock, descended slowly from his cab. He started to search for the inevitable mutilated body. What happened next we have no idea as we legged it.

Forgiven?

Anonymous.

Dear Father Simon,

I would like to confess to an incident that happened last year. I met my girlfriend in 1990 and within a few months, I decided to move out of London to live with her in Worcester.

At the time, we had two cars, my old Monza and her beautiful green 2CV – her pride and joy. Later in the year, she was given a company car, and she gave me her car for Christmas, with strict instructions to look after it and always keep it topped up with oil and water. This I promised faithfully I would do. I sold my car then suddenly her firm went under and she lost her new car.

To take her mind off it, I decided to drive her down to London for a weekend. We got in the car, and were driving down the motorway when there was a loud bang and the engine started smoking. We took it to a garage where the mechanic took one look at it and pursed his lips – which meant it was going to bad news. It was. The big end had gone.

Just one of those things, he told her. We weren't in the AA so my girlfriend rang her younger sister to tow us back to Worcester. When we got home, her mother offered to lend us her Citroen AX which had only done a handful of miles. So we set off again, almost five hours late.

As we passed the spot on the motorway we had broken down, a pheasant flew into the car. My girlfriend managed to keep control but on inspection, we realized the spoiler had been ripped off, the wheel trim was wrecked and there was blood everywhere. When we got to London, she spent the whole weekend wondering how she would break the news to her mother. Needless to say, her mother was not happy but after my girlfriend pointed out it was sheer bad luck that the big end had gone and not her fault, things calmed down.

I would now like to confess to the fact that luck played no part whatsoever, and that in fact it was all my fault. I had forgotten to put oil in the car since I had it, and as a result the engine was bone dry! No wonder the big end had gone.

I would like to ask forgiveness from my girlfriend Romany (now my wife), her sister who ended up towing us 60 miles back (never having towed anyone before), my new mother-in-law for wrecking her car and the mechanic – who knew exactly what had happened but took pity on me when I told him not to say anything as I was going to propose to my girlfriend very shortly.

Am I forgiven?

Simon.

Dear Father Simon,

I am writing to you to confess on behalf of a friend.

He was driving along one day in his pride and joy when a thrusting salesman Red XR3i cut him up so badly that he had to take evasive action, causing him to collide with a garden wall, thereby bending and scratching his front wing.

Much to my friend's surprise and chagrin, the XR3i didn't stop but sped off at some speed. Fortunately his car was not too badly damaged and so he gave chase, intent on 'discussing' the incident with the driver. As he caught the XR3i he realized the driver was not alone, but in the company of three rather large friends. Realizing that in the circumstances he was unlikely to be able to bring the XR3i driver around to his viewpoint, and deciding that discretion was the finer part of valour, he abandoned the chase, but took note of the car's registration number.

As it happened he saw a policeman friend the next day who offered to get the name and address of the driver from his mates in the traffic

police. Well, my friend had heard nothing for six weeks or so and was driving home a slightly different way when he saw the XR3i in a house drive. He checked the number, and, yes, it was the same car.

That night he took his revenge on the car, smashing all the glass, mirrors and lights with a hammer. Feeling justice had been done he went home to find his policeman friend had left a message on his answerphone. Apparently, the XR3i had been sold a couple of weeks before to someone living in the address he had just visited . . .

So, if you were that person and your new car was mysteriously vandalized in the middle of the night for no apparent reason, he is sorry and begs your forgiveness . . .

Is he forgiven?

Yours,
Otis.

Dear Father Simon,
My confession is in connection with a Saturday delivery job I used to do many moons ago at a very well-known bakers.

At the time all my mates had jobs there and with all of us not having passed our driving tests for long, it was very much the place to be on a Saturday morning . . . to learn just how high an engine could rev and how fast you could go round corners without the cream cakes ending up looking like, well, I'd rather not say.

One particular cold Saturday morning about 5.30 am there was talk in the yard of a new craze -- driving along at speed, switch the ignition off, pump the throttle, and switch the ignition back on. The result of igniting unburnt petrol made a loud bang from the exhaust. Oh what fun seeing old grannies jump about six feet in the air whilst waiting at bus stops.

My confession is about one of the lads who nearly got the sack and a criminal record. It was common knowledge at the time that he used to stop in at his girlfriend's house in Hatfield on his way back from a delivery. It just so happened that round the corner from her house was a mate of mine who looked after a community centre. I wondered just for a laugh if he would also jump six feet in the air when subject to a loud backfire!

Bright and very early the next Saturday I set off on my first delivery. Grinning from ear to ear I pulled into the community centre car park, switching the ignition off, then pumping the throttle, choke and everything else I could find, and carried out several backfires: the equivalent to Concorde breaking the sound barrier.

Needless to say I was rapidly on my way and feeling very pleased with myself. My evil grin was soon to disappear when I got back to the yard at the sight of two police cars leaving and a lot of shouting from the manageress. On enquiring what was happening I discovered that a resident had reported hearing several blasts from a shotgun and seen a white baker's van speedily leaving the area. The same area as my mate's girlfriend's house.

I will never forget the blank expression on his face for getting the blame, whilst not knowing what the heck was happening.

For this I ask to be forgiven and a thousand apologies to all those old grannies and especially the postie on his bike!

Yours remorsefully,
James.

P.S. Backfiring should not be practiced as it blows holes in the exhaust and can make worrying noises come from the engine – not to mention that the steering lock comes on when the ignition is switched off (this was a touch worrying when speeding through town centres) . . . Well, at least not in your own vehicle.

6

The Joy of Getting Even

I never liked the Deathwish movies. You could not describe Charles Bronson, even with one of his magnums pointed at your head, as a great contribution to the human race. 'Ah yes!' you Thatcherite children cry, 'but he got results.' He has clearly inspired this next collection of part-time vigilantes. Natural justice, Mr Bronson would call it, if he uses words that long.

Dear Father Mayo,

We are three young ladies who work for Abbey National at the Regional Office in Coventry, and feel compelled to write to you on behalf of a friend of ours. She is too embarrassed to write in herself and so let's call her Prudence (Pru to her friends).

After a hard day's work in the office, Pru went to catch her bus home. As she had a few minutes to spare she decided to get a drink at Pool Meadow Cafe. She bought a cup of coffee and a Kit Kat and went to sit down. The cafe was packed and there was no free tables, so she sat down opposite a young fella. She was half-way through her drink when he reached over, picked up her Kit Kat, broke off a piece and ate it!!! She was horrified and snatched it back and quickly ate a piece herself.

A few minutes passed when he again reached over, broke off another piece and starting eating it. She couldn't believe her eyes so she scoffed the rest before he had the chance. Without saying a word he went to the counter bought a huge cream cake and sat at another table.

Well, she wasn't going to let him get away with that! Upon seeing her bus pull in she raced over, picked up his cream cake and shoved as much as possible into her mouth and ran out. She reached the bus stop, feeling well pleased with herself, cream cake smeared all over her face. She reached into her bag and – yes you guessed it – there was her Kit Kat!!! She had put it into her bag when she had been at the counter, so the other one was the fella's all along.

She has never forgiven herself since, and she wants him to know she really did think it was her Kit Kat. Can he also find it in his heart to forgive her for scoffing his cream cake?

Love and Kisses,
Kirsty, Jo and Leanne.

Dear Father Simon,

In the late 1970s I won a scholarship to a local public school. Being local I attended as a 'dayer' and went home each evening. Luckily most of my house were in the same position and we all got on rather well.

As is usual in any class-ridden society (and our school was renowned for producing 'Gentlemen') we were looked down on by the boys whose families boarded their sons. The leader of the opposition was a particularly big-headed boy whom we shall call Rupert, and it was from him that most of the insults and practical jokes came.

We put up with this for five years, and it was not until the sixth form annual rugby match that we got our own back. I must explain that Rupert's parents were due to attend as the event was the last great bash before we broke for Christmas. His pa was due to donate the required funds to build the school a new science block so the masters told us to go easy on Rupert for the sake of the school.

The great day came and Rupert's parents arrived with as much fuss as is usually lavished on the Queen's corgies. His mother was dressed in all her Sunday best with a full-length Arctic fox fur coat which was rumoured to have cost more than the proposed science block.

The first half went without a hitch and we were winning, but more surprising was that Rupert's kit was still as clean as when he had put it on. To be truthful, he hadn't actually touched the ball by that stage and wouldn't have known what to do with it anyway. About half-way through the second half, in a complete lapse of concentration on the opposition's part, Rupert got the ball. Standing in the centre of the pitch he was rooted to the spot wondering what to do, when the combined weight of our front row hit him at full speed. I won't describe the extent of the scene, but needless to say Rupert had been buried.

The scene was further complicated by Rupert's mother running onto the field shouting her head off. By this time the action had moved on and we were running the ball up field. To this day I don't know how it happened, but out of the corner of my eye I saw someone in white obviously unmarked calling for the ball. I passed it and Rupert's mother caught it. Like her son before her, she, too, stopped dead in her tracks.

Unfortunately the opposition, seeing the ball in our hands, proceeded to give her the Rupert treatment. The amazing thing was that none of the surrounding mud seemed to miss her and the coat was ruined.

The headmaster stopped the game and both mother and son were carted off to the sick bay looking slightly the worse for wear. The consequence of our actions was that the school didn't get the promised science lab. The money was probably spent on a new coat, and Rupert's two brothers were removed from the school.

I would like to apologize to the school for the loss of both science block and school fees. And would like to say to Rupert's mother, serves you right for wearing such a cruel piece of wardrobe and dragging up such a loathesome son.

Forgiven?

Steve.

Dear Simon

I have a confession to make which shows the devious nature I possess. One of my friends may get a bit of a shock, but I don't care anymore. He never questioned me about the incident and I am sure he has always secretly suspected me.

We have grown up together and my friend has increasingly annoyed me by sending things to my address with my name on them. I am referring to things such as catalogues, British Telecom info, Family Planning advice, every privatization prospectus ever published, and so on. The final straw was when I received an information pack about becoming a sperm donor which I inadvertently opened in front of my parents who have looked at me differently ever since.

This called for immediate action because I was going on holiday in a week so I started to look for some sort of suitable revenge. I found the answer in my friendly Yellow Pages and soon my fingers were doing the talking. I also noted down a few numbers to take on holiday with me.

The day I awaited arrived and I got up early to make a few phone calls using the phone on the caravan site in France. The result of these calls was that an emergency plumber, an electrician and a roof repairer arrived at my friend's house at approximately 5.30 am and demanded to be paid vast sums of money for arriving as early as they had been asked to. It took about an hour for them to be sent away. Not long after that two trucks arrived and proceeded to dump a ton of sand and a ton of gravel onto their front garden. The two truck drivers had long gone when the family rose from their sleep to find the materials covering their garden. It took them 45 minutes of heated phone conversations to find the companies that had delivered the materials and arrange for them to come and take them away again which cost about £40 altogether.

At about 12 o'clock in France I made several phone calls again to England to give my friend and his family a bit of a treat. Sure enough they were duly presented with eight family sized pizzas from local take-away establishments. Apparently they ate the first two but sent the others away. Then it was the turn of the mini-skips to turn up at their house as I had prearranged – but by now they were getting the hang of dissuading people from leaving their objects outside the house. Consequently not one of the six skips was left at their house.

Four o'clock British time saw the arrival of 12 different taxis that had all been arranged to pick up my friend and drive him to a place 70 miles away. I had, however, not taken the taxi driver's attitudes into consideration when they thought they were losing their best fare of the week to another driver. A scuffle broke out and two of the drivers were arrested by the police who had been alerted by a neighbour. They were later released with just a warning when the circumstances were made clear.

The crowning glory of my revenge was the visit by the local commercial radio station (naff FM) who were intrigued by the claim that my friend's parrot could do multiplication and shout out the answers. Unfortunately there was no parrot and instead the rather agitated family told the researchers about their ordeal and made it onto the radio that way. (This amused all three of the station's listeners.)

As I was on holiday I was not under any suspicion and the people who got the blame from my friend were the others he had sent useless literature to. I do not ask forgiveness for my act which I rather enjoyed (it kept me chuckling for weeks) and it cost me a lot (!) of money to phone from France. I do however ask forgiveness for making those three men get out of bed for no reason, for making my friend's parents pay to have the stuff removed from their garden, for ruining their garden and for getting two men arrested for fighting for their business.

Yours sincerely,
Matthew.

Dear Father Mayo,

We feel it is time to confess to our terrible sin that we committed about a year ago.

It all began when one of us was seeing who she thought was 'Mr Right', although I thought this smarmy, pretentious creep was 'Mr Wrong'. His name was George and he worked in the offices of a computer showroom, although he kept bragging he was worth much more. He had applied for a particular job with a well-known High Street bank, which would bring him promotion and better pay.

He had attended an interview and was sure he was the best man for the job. Now he had achieved greater status in his career he felt my friend was no longer good enough for him, and went as far as telling her so. This obviously left her upset and wanting revenge – so we started plotting.

The next day I rang George explaining that I was the personnel manager from the branch 'he would be working at'. I went on to tell him he had got the job and to hand in his notice at the firm he currently worked at, as he would start work in three weeks time. I also told him to buy suitable clothes and preferably a real leather briefcase. He would start work at 10.30 am and so was asked to arrive at the front desk at 10 am to introduce himself to the manager.

In the weeks that followed we discovered he had immediately given up his job in favour of his 'new career'. We also learned he had been spending his nights in, saving up for a new suit and a real leather briefcase, costing around £200.

About 9.55 am on the morning George was due to start his new job, it just so happened we had run out of money so we called in at our local bank. Just before 10 am the doors opened and there was George, modelling a brand new designer suit and clutching a leather briefcase. As we hid behind the leaflets he confidently strode to the front desk and asked for the manager.

When the manager appeared George shook him firmly by the hand and loudly announced himself as the new management trainee due to start today. The bewildered bank manager made his excuses to check this, leaving a less-confident George nervously clutching his briefcase.

The bank manager's reappearance confirmed that George had been mistaken and the job was not his after all. After much argument with him, George was repeatedly told that it was a good application but the job had gone to someone else. George was then requested to leave.

We would like to confess to the bank manager – yes, it was those two giggling girls behind the mortgage leaflets that had played the prank. We would also like to confess to George, that it was us and we are very sorry you lost both jobs, your social life, your savings, your dignity and your pride, (still the leather briefcase does look nice whilst you collect your UB40).

But most of all we would like to apologize to the bank 'that likes to say YES' – but this time said NO.

Can we be forgiven for our sin as we brought pleasure and amusement to a few bored cashiers and customers in that bank on that morning?

From,
Two little angels.

Dear Father Simon,

I have something to confess and I beg your absolution from this heinous crime. It happened some years ago now in my home town. My elder brother, a tall and muscular bloke, was involved in the local rugby team which had just bought a new kit. Being younger, I was not as well built, but since I was just as tall, tended to be one of those people described as 'lanky', much to the ridiculing of my elder brother.

After the second game of the season, which my brother's team won easily, putting them on top of the division, so they celebrated in my local pub. My brother started shouting across the pub at me and generally taking the mick. Since I was the butt of the entire rugby team's jokes and they were larger and greater in number than me and the few friends I was with, I couldn't reek my revenge there. However . . . I was prepared to wait.

During this waiting in the pub I did what is usually done in pubs until my sense of fairplay was drowned. When time was called my brother and the team left just before I did. I strolled outside minutes later to see my brother being given the kit to wash since he lived nearest. He took the kit, which at the beginning of the day had been a white top, red shorts and red socks and was now generally black, home much to our Mother's disgust. She was not happy at the prospect of our washing machine being used to wash such a filthy kit. After explaining to him how to make the washing machine come on in the early hours so it would be cheaper and telling him to boil wash the whites separately, she went to bed.

My brother loaded up the washing machine with the white tops, set it on boil and set it to start washing at 4 am. He then went upstairs and fell into a drunken slumber. I'm sure something happens to people's brains when they watch late night TV, it's all rubbish but you sit there as though it's the best stuff ever. My Dad went to bed and I pretended I really wanted to watch the next programme which was about the Indonesian Top 10 or some such rubbish.

Once Dad was in bed I crept through to the kitchen, opened up the washing machine and shoved in as many of the red socks and shorts as I could. I then poured in some red food colouring and some red ink my Dad had in his desk (my Dad being a teacher), closed the door again, then went to bed and fell into my drunken slumber.

I was woken next morning by the birds singing gently in the trees, the church bells calling people to worship, my brother yelling 'What the hell happened here?' and then cursing his headache. I strolled casually downstairs and asked what was happening. My Mum pointed out of the window where I saw my brother hanging out decidedly pink rugby tops and slightly faded red shorts and socks. Despite his best efforts he couldn't restore the shirts to their former glory and so the team had to play in a pink and red/faded strip for the rest of the season.

I do not ask forgiveness from the rugby team nor my brother but from two sources. Firstly my parents for using their red dyes, and secondly, the fans of the team (only about a dozen people) because they could no longer shout for their red and white army and had to face being the supporters of a team called the Pink Flamingos by everyone else.

Yours Pleadingly,
Neill.

Dear Simon Mayo,

My confession happened a couple of years ago while I was working for a computer installation company.

I was in charge of a team of engineers who were laying a new network into a building near the sea front one summer weekend. All week one of the guys from another region had been winding us up with his stories of excellence: his fancy qualifications, his ability to fix a problem almost before it happened and so on. His only failing seemed to be that he was red/green colour blind.

On the way in that morning I picked up a couple of the men and our conversation swung towards this fine view we should have of that morning's special event at the power station. As we chatted a plot hatched whereby we could have some revenge. When we arrived at work one of the men spent a couple of hours laying a bogus cable to perfectly position a junction box on the wall just under a window with a view to the power station.

It was my job to convince the expert that he had the most important job of wiring up the final multi-core cable to the box. I quickly filled him in on what was to be done and pointed out two red and green cables which must not, under any circumstances be joined. We left him to it just before 12.00 noon, apparently to pop round the corner to collect fish and chips. In truth we wanted to get a good view of what was to happen.

At noon precisely there was an almighty explosion. The East chimney of the derelict power station a few hundred yards away was demolished. We knew it was set off by the winner of a local competition. Our expert did not. He must have been coming to the red and green wires just at that time because when we returned to the room all that was left was his wire stripper and screwdriver where they had tumbled under the joint box.

Maybe it was embarrassment or maybe he really believed that he had caused the chimney to fall but he never returned to work with us again.

Colin.

Dear Simon and the Breakfast Crew,

Many years ago I was a medical secretary at a hospital and worked on one of the wards. We often used to receive presents such as huge boxes of choccies and biscuits from patients, which we used to devour as quickly as possible. One of the ward nurses was one of those infuriating people who could stuff chocolate until the cows came home and never put on an ounce. She was like a stick insect.

So one day a fellow fattie colleague and I decided to get our own back. We had been given a particularly huge box of choccies from a nice elderly gentleman patient. My colleague procured some local anaesthetic which we proceeded to inject into our thin friend's favourite centres. We then told her we'd had enough and that she could eat the rest – which she did.

Five minutes passed. She said her mouth felt a bit dry and went to get a cup of tea. We could hardly contain ourselves as we watched the tea pour back out of her mouth and down the front of her nice white uniform – and we knew the doctors would be round in about one minute's time. She was horrified to find her mouth had gone completely numb. After realizing that she couldn't possibly have contracted foot and mouth disease she calmed down and came to the conclusion that she must have accidently touched her mouth after handling anaesthetic. We reassured her this must have been the case.

I'm not really sorry because it was so funny – but are we forgiven?

Yours sincerely,
'A reformed Chocoholic'.

Dear Crew,

I feel I must confess to you, mainly on someone else's behalf. I am guilty too, but only of the sin of schadenfreude – malicious pleasure in another's misfortune.

Once upon a time many years ago I lived in a shared house, you know the sort of thing – 15 impoverished junior civil servants and bank clerks sharing a variable number of bedrooms, a bathroom and kitchen. No one ever cleans the bath, and the fridge is full of containers half-full of green fur, with the name of the bloke who moved out six weeks ago written on the side so no one is going to touch them.

It happened that one of our jolly band, Malcolm, was universally detested by the rest. Well, he was a bit of a plank, or rather two not very tall ones. Malc had recently destroyed my pressure cooker by moving it to the super heat ring on the stove, so he could heat his tin of beans, and leaving it for two hours.

Soon after this episode, another of our number, Jim, was making wine, a particularly delicious (strong) concoction of grape and banana. Jim had boiled up the grape concentrate with a large number of mashed bananas and strained the liquid out using the largest sieve we had. He was on his way to the bin outside the back door with the remaining revolting mess when he tripped on the back step. The mess slopped into a steaming, lumpy puddle just outside the door.

At this point, Malcolm walked into the yard. 'Look at this,' Jim said, 'isn't it disgusting, someone's been sick on our doorstep.' Malcolm turned a bit pale, then Jim bent down to the puddle and stuck his finger in it, exclaiming, 'They can't have got far – it's still warm!' Malc turned green, and as Jim raised his finger to his lips and turned to enquire, 'Who's been eating bananas?' Malcolm fled, hand over mouth.

I beg forgiveness for Jim, whose quick wit wreaked delightful revenge, and for myself, because I revelled in it. I also ask you to spare some sympathy for poor Malcolm who couldn't really help his *plankishness and moved out soon after, before the wine was even ready to drink.*

Mea culpa,
Sara.

Dear Simon and Squad,

The blame for this letter is all yours, for your confessions spot inspired me to play my prank.

Over two years ago I left university but wanted to 'bum it' a little so since then I have enjoyed myself doing casual labour at home and abroad – such as bar work in Spain, time-share selling in Tenerife, and hotel work in Portugal. This year I have had a great time labouring on a sheep farm in Wales. Although the farmer was a real pain his daughter Sally was a good laugh and we enjoyed working together. In my spare time both the local pub and curry house was a real favourite and I made a close friendship with the son of the Indian restaurant's owner.

One evening I commented to him that the pale pink and yellow rice looked nice and he said that only a very tiny pinch of colouring was needed to tint a whole cauldron of rice. Well the plot hatched. Since I and Tommy (another labourer on the farm) were to shortly begin sheep dipping on the flock, my Indian friend agreed to nick a large tin of red colouring from his Dad.

The day came and all chemical preparations were made. I told Tommy I had forgotten the prodding stick and whilst he went to get it I poured all the colouring into the murky grey water. The sheep bleeted and scampered through the solution and came out of the dip what can only be described as wet with a very dull brownish tint. Well, I was a little disappointed, but around the one hundreth sheep as they began to dry out Tommy yelled look at the sheep. I smiled because the sun had dried the sheep to, no not a pink, but more of a bright luminouis fuchsia colour.

I told Tommy it must be a new type of dip which indicated which sheep you had done so you didn't do some twice. He fell for that. As you can imagine Sally's Dad went bananas and blamed a very famous chemical company for a batch of faulty dipping solution, and was threatening legal action against them.

The best was yet to come. When the local villagers got to know of the bright pink sheep, they came in droves to peer over his wall which made Sally's Dad completely lose his marbles. He even stopped going to the local for a beer. One day a passing coach stopped at the corner field and the whole busload got off to have a closer look. They soon moved on when I said they turned that colour just after the Chernobyl incident.

Well, I soon moved on from Wales and am now working on a building site although my contract will be ended in two weeks, I never found out who got the blame and didn't bother to leave a forwarding address.

Yours,
Cheers Mike.

P.S. Dianne'd better forgive me or I'll send her some bath oil for Christmas which may be heavy in colouring.

P.P.S. Before I left I intended to paint a sign at the entrance 'Jervez, sheep permed and tinted at reasonable prices,' but I felt I had done enough!

Simon,
I would like to apologize to four people.

On the building site where I was working at the time, the prat of a site manager had a lovely morning giving me a verbal dressing down in front of half the workforce so revenge was on my mind. The idea came to me that he was due to show some prospective buyers around one of the luxury flats.

I spied a young apprentice leaning out of the window of the flat as these two elderly women were about to be shown around. These windows were the dropleaf type so it was easy for me to creep up behind him and jam his head outside the window by wedging a piece of wood between the windows leaving the rest of him inside.

I then proceeded to lower his trousers and boxer shorts and also to slap a bit of white gloss on each buttock. 'A lovely view from this window' were the words I then heard coming from the hall. It was the great salesman himself.

I slipped into a wardrobe and listened to four screams: one from the site manager when he opened the door, two from the dear old ladies who walked out in disgust and the biggest from the young lad with his head out of the window and his white bum inside the room.

Being the person I am I stayed inside the wardrobe sniggering until the heat had died down. I daresay the site manager did not get his sales commission that day.

So can I say 'sorry' and beg forgiveness especially from the young lad who never did quite get on with the site manager from that day on, and to the two elderly women.

Expecting forgiveness,
Pete.

7

Animal Magic

You know you have a winning confession when the BBC's duty log starts to fill up with complaints from irate listeners. You are about to read the stories that provoke 90 per cent of them. You have two choices. Either fall about with mirth (like me) or ring 071-580 4468 – The Duty Officer has heard it all before.

Dear All,

Hearing you talking about maggots on your show prompts me to write to you about something that has not really been on my conscience very much, but you might enjoy it.

On or about 1967, when I was but 15 years of age, several friends and I used to catch a train from south-east London to Maidstone to do a spot of juvenile fishing (lobbing bricks at each others floats and so on). On our way there we were in a railway carriage in which the seats were arranged back to back, with the netting luggage rack above. I'm sure you know the sort. While peeping over the top, to see what we could see, we were happy to see a sweet old biddy wearing a wide-brimmed hat with an upturned rim. She didn't see us, or hear our silent titters, as she had her back to us. There was no one else in view.

The hat, we thought, would be an excellent circular race track for our maggots. Round and round they went! My one was hell bent on winning, but just near the post, the train slowed up and stopped at Maidstone Station. It was the sweet old biddy's stop! Off she got, stealing our maggots into the bargain. The cheek of it!

I'd like to apologize to my maggot as it would have won the 'Order of the Barbed Hook' for coming first . . . and I'd like to apologize to the sweet little old biddy who walked around Maidstone High Street on a busy Saturday with maggots racing around her bonce.

Am I forgiven? Actually I don't really mind if I'm not as it made our day.

All the best,
Peter.

Dear Simon,

As a student of the local college – some years ago – money was short, so to supplement one's drinking habits a part-time job was required. Now due to the large number of students, jobs were in short supply, so it was to my Gran I turned for inspiration. Dog walking was the idea she came up with – pointing out that from her group of friends, we had a ready-made client bank.

The idea was that I'd walk the dogs twice a day, for half an hour, three times a week, for a nominal fee. Everyone was happy and all went smoothly for two weeks, but as with many jobs the boredom set in. Same dogs, same route and it was starting to take it's toll on my legs and patience.,

Then an idea struck me. Shorter, faster walks would have better results. The dogs would be fitter – and I'd have more time to myself – yet I'd still earn the dough. With this in mind I took to taking the dogs for a walk alongside me as I cycled. I could go at some speed and the dogs managed to keep up – well almost!

Now at this stage I must point out that my grandmother is aged 79 and as her friends are of around the same age, the dogs are no spring chickens either. So as I look back now – I realize the error of my ways.

Duke, a lovely Irish setter who loved a run, was the first to go. At least that was how it seemed. He followed the bike, his tongue hanging out – happily lolloping behind – or maybe his tongue was hanging out because I was pedalling at around 40 miles an hour. Poor Duke limped home, and when I went to call for him the next day he refused to budge. His owner was bewildered – Duke had always liked a walk – but just put his subsequent rheumatism down to old age.

The much faster and much shorter walks started to take their toll. We had four dogs down in the space of three weeks, but I'd made my money so it was time to call it a day before any more dodgy doggy dilemmas occurred.

Only one owner insisted I couldn't let her down. Her labrador, Penny, needed a walk – I couldn't mess people around this way. All right – Penny would get her run – boy did she run! 'Was it a bird – was it a plane?' No it was Penny the Labrador. Like a streak of lightning, feet barely touching the ground as she hurtled along behind my bike. She went home exhausted but I didn't care as I was never going to call on her owner again.

Being a loving grandson, I called at Granny's house the next day to be faced with the news. Penny the unlucky labrador had died in the night! Granny said she knew why I was so distressed 'Yes – it's so easy to get attached to a lovely dog like that but the vet said old age catches up with all of us eventually!!'

Well I'd got away with it – but ever since – my heart has been heavy. Now I'm not a man to argue with a professional's opinion – the vet obviously knows more about animals than I do – but just in case – Simon, am I forgiven?

Anonymous.

Dear Simon,

This confession goes back to 1964. I was 14 years old and living near Guildford. The person to whom I must confess is my sister, June, who to this day thinks her pet hamster 'Hammy' disappeared by escaping from his cage in our dining room. 'Wrong'

At this time I was very engrossed in radio-controlled model aircraft and I used to go to a local cricket ground with a friend to fly my latest acquisition, a three-channel 60″ wingspan 'KeilKraft Matador'. The actual cricket pitch made a perfect smooth take off and landing strip for the aircraft and I soon became very proficient at the controls.

After a while we became bored and started placing model soldiers and other such items inside the cockpit.

Now there was a television programme called 'Tales of the Riverbank' for younger viewers which featured a hamster which, amongst other things, used to be seen driving a jeep and a boat. So I thought, I wonder if Hammy would like a flight in my aeroplane.

On further discussion with my friend we duly selected a shoe box complete with holes in both ends and transported Hammy and my aeroplane – which had a large cockpit area, plenty of room for Hammy – to the cricket ground. We popped him in, complete with carrots, and, after starting up, taxied him down the runway ready for take-off.

My friend and I lay down on the ground when he went past to get a proper perspective of his size and make the whole flight more realistic. We could see Hammy sitting up looking out through the cockpit window. After three or four circuits of the playing fields I landed him and he was still looking out through the cockpit having obviously enjoyed the whole trip.

This little treat for Hammy was repeated on several more occasions. Until one day, after having taken off, the aeroplane was coming towards us, nice and low for a flypast when I suddenly noticed a distinct slackness in the controls. I made the aircraft turn and bank away in a large arc and on its second flypast I lost radio control altogether. Hammy passed for the last time over our heads, still gazing intently through the front screen, obviously still enjoying himself unaware of the pending disaster.

My continued efforts of frantically prodding the controls for some response were alas to no avail, the aircraft and Hammy continued to climb steadily away into the sunset until it was literally in the clouds and then out of sight. After the shock of losing my aeroplane my thoughts turned to my sister. She adored Hammy, what was I to do? After some thought I staged a 'breakout' from the hamster cage. That wire is really tough stuff when you try to chomp it with wire cutters to look like it was teeth but, with a little sawdust scattered on the floor, the stage was set.

The final result was very convincing and imagine my relief when my father told my broken-hearted and by now sobbing sister that it was quite common for hamsters to gnaw through wire in this fashion and that Hammy had probably gone out the back door and is now living back with nature.

I'm very sorry and I am glad to have told someone else about the poor hamster's demise.

Yours sincerely,
Keith.

Uh-uh! Wouldn't surprise me! What was it you used to do to your wee brother's teddy?!

Dear Simon,

I write to beg forgiveness for the following confession which took place back in 1989.

At the time I was working in Oxfordshire and playing rugby for one of the local clubs. We were a fairly strong team but had one feared opposition. The club in question was one of those that prided itself on how well-drilled the team was, and this extended off the pitch into the changing rooms where the club coach would hang up all the team's shirts, shorts, jockstraps, socks and boots prior to the game.

The dreaded game approached and, since our team were disheartened prior to the encounter, we knew we were in for a massive loss. The day dawned, and, sure enough, the opposition coach turned up to place the kit in the changing room before the team arrived. Two colleagues and myself saw our chance. We 'borrowed' the club's duplicate keys and let ourselves into the empty opposition changing room carrying several tubes of extra-strong Deep Heat. We then proceeded to rub a quantity into every jockstrap pouch in that

room – Deep Heat being a liniment rub that causes intense heat to the area it is applied to help the repair of muscles, should never be applied to sensitive areas.

The opposition arrived and got changed. Their team warm-up must have been a treat to watch as the Deep heat warmed up the parts other warm-ups cannot reach. Eventually some of them found their way out on to the pitch, peering through tear-filled eyes while others were vigorously scrubbing themselves in the showers in a manner that would have embarrassed the most debauched rugby player, and their coach was screaming that his team had been got at, something completely denied by our club officials.

Eventually all their players took to the field, still in some considerable pain, and the game started. After about the third scrum-down our team got used to the overpowering smell of Deep Heat and set about grinding the opposition into the ground. This was not too difficult considering the opposition seemed somewhat subdued, and less than willing to get involved.

I wish to confess that their discomfort was indeed due to our club, or at least three of its members, and that is possibly why they did not play with their normal aggression and commitment, thereby losing the match.

How about total absolution?

Yours sincerely,
Alexander.

Dear Simon,

I felt I should write and confess – not on my own behalf – but for my cousin.

Terry is a respected member of the community, a school governor, member of the local church, works for an insurance company (say no more) and a great animal lover (although it is hard to believe sometimes). His daughter, Michaela, was given a hamster for a birthday present, who was duly named George. All the books were read on hamster care, and he was given all the things hamsters need.

One day approximately one year ago, Michaela announced that George had died. There followed a period of mourning, and then it was decided he should be buried. Terry was appointed as undertaker and he duly removed George to the chosen spot in the garden. As Terry began to dig his grave, he noticed that George was moving. Terry, being the compassionate sort, to end his suffering decided to finish him off.

It not only ended his suffering, but also ended George, because he was actually just having a little snooze for the cold winter months, and would have lived to see another spring had he been given the chance.

I, therefore, ask for forgiveness on behalf of Terry from George and hamsters everywhere.

Yours sincerely,
Stephen.

8

The Parts That Other Confessions Cannot Reach

Proof, if it were needed that playground humour is alive and well, and flourishing all the way to the staff room and beyond. Just the mention of jockstraps, bosoms, and toilet seats seems to be enough to send the nation into giggles of appreciation. The spirit of Benny Hill appears to be with us still.

Dear Father Mayo,
I am writing to you on behalf of my fiancé, who I shall call 'Colin'.

The story begins some years ago when Colin went to Northallerton, a nearby town, to do the weekly shopping. After parking the car and heading at full speed to the nearest supermarket he decided he needed the toilet, so he popped into the brand-new, all-singing, all-dancing Supaloo just down the road. On entering, he was rather surprised to find only one urinal, but nevertheless began to do what he had to do. He then became aware somebody else had come in behind him, and looking over his shoulder, Colin saw another man just standing there staring at him.

As you may imagine, my fiancé began to get a little worried, so he quickly zipped himself up and left. The following week Colin was in Northallerton again, and once more felt the call of nature. He dutifully trooped off to the new loos, walked inside – and then stopped in horror as he saw a man who appeared to be drinking at the 'urinal'.

With a sudden uneasy feeling he checked around the next corner of the corridor and yes! There, neatly lined up, was a whole row of toilets, specially-designed for doing what Colin had done in the drinking fountain the week before. Meanwhile, some poor bloke was drinking away, oblivious to the situation.

On behalf of Colin I would like to apologize to this man, and also to North Yorkshire County Council for polluting their drinking water supply.

Is he forgiven?

Anonymous.

Dear Father Mayo, Sister Dianne and Pope Rod,
I beg forgiveness for the following act which involved a major chainstore and a changing room! This August whilst frantically searching for the ultimate sexy and slimming swimming costume three hours before going on holiday, I found a cheap reasonable costume and a bikini. Both looked like they might do the trick.

A friend accompanied me into the changing room to rest her weary legs. Being a modest young lady, I wanted to reveal the bare minimum of my white lardy body to my friend. Having tried on the costume that made me look like an Orange – cellulite skin thrown in, I manoeuvred into the bikini top with what I felt subtle, unrevealing movements.

All was well. I had the bikini top on with the pumpkin like costume still on my bottom. I was contemplating the top and showing off the graceful form of my bust, when it became too much of a strain for the clasp at the back and it promptly twanged off! This horror was too much for us both. Our nervous reaction was full-blown hysterics, which, in my case, soon developed a further nervous reaction. Within seconds our laughter was drowned out by the fountain of my natural fluids! Not just a dribble but a cascade equatable with the Niagara Falls.

The plastic hygiene liner in the costume could not cope with the torrent, and it soaked through my knickers, and on to the changing room floor (where my jeans and shoes lay, drowning). Thankfully the carpet was ultra-absorbent.

After 15 minutes of whispered and hysterical conferring, we decided I couldn't buy it because a) it was hideous and b) the counter staff would have seen my unfortunate accident. I eventually walked out, calmly clutching the costume in my hand, pretending I was going to buy it. We then proceeded to place it back on the rack and walk out of the store!

I ask forgiveness from the sweet-looking lad who was in charge of the changing room and didn't say a thing despite our laughter and whispering, and the person who may have bought the soiled article. Am I forgiven?

Anonymous.

P.S. I can hardly bring myself to confess that a similar incident occurred two years before in the same store with a cocktail dress, only then my friend joined me in my incontinent activities! Am I still forgiven?

Dear Simon & Crew

As you will recall the summer of '76 was a hot one, ideal conditions for D.I.Y. and general renovations to one's house – at least this was the thinking of my uncle, who was undertaking to do just that to the cloakroom and toilet at the back of his house. As it was during the summer holidays my cousin, a number of friends and myself were eager to lend a hand.

I was given the job, much to the dismay of my cousin I might add, of sanding down and refurbishing an antique wooden toilet seat. This I did with enthusiasm. With all the help, and good weather all was soon completed. My uncle was especially pleased with the job I'd done with the toilet seat – sanded and varnished looking as good as new. Although pleased with my efforts I felt a further coat of varnish would further enhance the look of the said seat, so I took it upon myself to do just that – with, I might add, no prompting or knowledge of my uncle, cousin or friends.

The next day we'd all arranged to meet up in the local park – but strangely my cousin never turned up. Apparently he had taken it upon himself to further carry out decorations to his father's house namely 're-varnish' the toilet seat of the downstairs toilet – little known to his father who, thinking all was well, had in the usual manner taken advantage of his newly finished amenity.

It must be said at this time that my uncle can only be described as a very large man who is blessed with an unnatural amount of body hair!! It turned out that having positioned himself upon the said amenity with the newly varnished seat he'd become well and truly stuck – so much so that it took his wife and her mother twenty-five minutes, half a bottle of white spirit and lots of gentle sponging to remove the offending item from my uncle's nether regions, along with skin and a large amount of body hair.

My cousin had been blamed and was to be kept at home for the rest of the summer holidays and no pocket money. I now feel it is time to come clean – own up and seek forgiveness from my cousin – loss of holiday and money – my uncle – considerable discomfort – my auntie and her mother, the unending abuse they received whilst removing the 'sticky toilet seat'.

Am I forgiven?

Adam.

Dear Simon,

I feel compelled to write to you to ask for forgiveness, for a terrible deed I did nearly 10 years ago. It still haunts me, even though I have moved out of the area. Simon, I went unpunished for the crime; Fred my mate 'carried the can' and has suffered persecution, harassment and embarrassment ever since.

My local rugby club of Brecon were on tour to Portsmouth to play the Navy which had kindly put us up in its barracks. I was an innocent 17 year-old celebrating my birthday on what was my first tour. One of the older, respectable gents of the tour suggested a couple of drinks before we changed into collar and tie for the after-match reception. What a good idea, we said!

Whilst I was changing into my new suit, some evil fiend threw a cup of cold water over my new shirt. I was outraged – this was my 18th birthday, how dare they do this to me and spoil my day. I went looking for revenge. On searching the barrack bathroom area, I found one cubicle engaged and I assumed this must be where he was hiding. I found the mop bucket half-full of stagnant water and detergent and, after I finished with it a few other necessities, I picked it up, tip-toed to the cubicle, shouted 'This will teach you' and threw the bucket over. I then scarpered quick, passing Fred in the corridor.

On arrival at the reception there were many long faces. Some of the boys had gone down the pub and hadn't come back, maybe because I told them it started at 9.30 instead of 7.30, but worse was to come. Somebody had soaked the Mayor of Brecon in his official uniform with chain of office. He was also receiving medical treatment for a head injury sustained by a flying bucket which had also blackened his eye.

I couldn't hold back. I had to say something, but it came out all wrong, I said, 'It was Fred. I passed him running in the corridor.' Fred couldn't defend himself as he was down the pub with the rest of the boys. They believed my story as I was too young to know any different. Brecon RFC paid the cleaning bill but the Mayor is now the Chairman of the rugby club and poor old Fred has suffered on every tour since, until now.

   Am I forgiven for this?

Yours faithfully,
Robert.

Dear Simon and the rest of the Breakfast Crew,

The dastardly deed occurred several years ago when I was a student living in Wales. My friend and his girlfriend came to visit my girlfriend and me for a few days in the summer. Now Rob was a good friend of mine, though Karen his girlfriend was annoying and had a reputation as a real flirt.

On the first night we went out for a meal. We sat so that my girlfriend sat opposite me and Karen on my left. Well you can imagine my surprise, despite my ugly looks, when Karen started to rub my thigh midway through the meal. So that I didn't upset everyone I quickly and quietly grabbed her hand and gave it an unfriendly squeeze and dropped it by her side.

The next day was blazing hot, quite unusual for Wales in Summer. We decided that we would head for the beach. Living locally I knew a secluded spot which was isolated from the main tourist areas. On arrival we all changed into our beach gear. Unfortunately my girlfriend's bikini, which she had bought the day before, had no stitching down one side of the bottoms rendering them useless. She decided it needed to go back.

As we had travelled to the beach in Rob's car he would have to drive as I was not insured for his company car and Rob was very car proud. I offered to go with them to town but Rob insisted on me staying as Karen was keen to make the most of the sun. Once Rob and my girlfriend left I settled down in the sand to soak up the sun. I was, however, apprehensive as I knew what Karen was like and that the others would be gone at least one-and-a-half-hours given the amount of tourist traffic. Within a few minutes she asked if I would rub some of her very strong sun block cream into her back as she could not reach and was particularly prone to burning with such fair skin. Reluctantly I agreed.

So that she didn't get a bikini line she had already undone her back strap. Annoyed at her as I knew this was a typical Karen come-on I fumbled reluctantly in the beach bag for the sun block. I then came across some hand cream in a similar tube as the sun block. It was at this point that the thought which led to the evil deed crossed my mind. I decided to get my own back for the night before and her being such a flirt behind my mate's back. I knew that while she was lying face down it was unlikely that she would detect the difference between the high factor sun block cream and the 'useless' hand cream.

As I rubbed the hand cream into her she commented on how smooth and yet masculine my hands were. Quickly I finished putting the cream onto her back and said, 'finished', grinning to myself at the effect my quick thinking would have on Karen's slightly bronzed, but still delicate, skin. At this point she turned over so that her bikini top fell off. She then asked if I would do her front. Trying to hide my embarrassment and not show my anger with her for expecting that I would make moves on my best friend's girlfriend, I said yes, as I could not help but notice her breasts were very white and had not seen the sun before that year.

She didn't notice I was rubbing hand cream into her front because the sun was making her squint. At that point I think she detected my resistance to her as she made no more immediate advances. Having finished I put the cream back in the beach bag and ran off to go for a swim.

During that morning she asked me three times to rub some more cream into her front. Each time she pushed her luck a little bit further. Fortunately Rob and my girlfriend turned up before she got totally out of control. By this time her blatant advances had convinced me I was right to have played this trick, thereby clearing my conscience and removing all my guilt.

It had taken over two hours for Rob and my girlfriend to return. During this time Karen had been lying on her back exposing her body. To say the effects were spectacular is an understatement. Karen was burnt all over. But her chest was so burnt it actually swelled up! Though, Rob told me this in confidence so I probably still shouldn't be telling you. But it must have been bad for she could not wear a bra as none of hers fitted.

Rob hit the roof with her for being so stupid as to get that burnt. He had to drive her home first thing the next day as she was so ill and wouldn't be treated by any of the local doctors. He left muttering something about Karen and huge red peppers. It ruined his plans for a dirty break and virtually finished their relationship which was never the same again. Rob and Karen have since split.

To this day they never found out what I did on the beach. The immediate effects of my actions were what I had hoped for, though I must admit that I did feel some guilt two months later when Rob explained his and other people's suffering due to Karen's 'accident'.

I would therefore like to ask forgiveness from my mate Rob whose dirty break and relationship was ruined, her doctor who had to face Karen the next day (and keep a straight face), the woman in the chemist shop who got a blasting from Karen about how poor their most expensive sun block cream was. I would also like to apologize to the company who produced the cream as I understand they got a nasty letter and apologetically sent Karen a considerable quantity of free creams as compensation. Lastly, I would like to ask forgiveness from Karen.

Simon I have changed the names of the injured parties in this sad story to save them any more embarrassment. I hope that this story meets with your approval and that I can be truly forgiven.

Yours anonymously,
Steven.

P.S. I have some other good stories but they will have to wait as I can't lose all my friends at once.

Dear Father Simon,

I am finally compelled to confess to a rather embarrassing little episode that happened to me a few years ago when driving home from work. I had been stuck in a jam on the M40 for quite some time, and so when I turned off onto the country roads (the M40 finished at Junction 7 then), I was rather in need of a comfort stop. However, the countryside of Oxfordshire is not over-blessed with service areas, but it does have some very quiet and secluded roads.

So it was that I found one such remote and deserted spot, complete with thick hedge, and proceeded to do what comes naturally. Imagine my distress when, just at a most awkward point in the process, I heard voices coming from a short distance along the road and some brightly coloured clothing came into view through the hedge. Not wishing to draw attention to the exposed part of my body, I turned away from the two people who were now climbing over the stile onto the road, and walked calmly towards my car which was fortunately facing the right direction. On climbing into the driving seat, I made a hasty attempt to adjust my trousers, but found to my horror that there was a problem with my zip.

I thought very quickly and reached for a map from my glove compartment, spread it on my lap, and proceeded to study it most intently as my fellow travellers passed by my car. I was just thanking my lucky stars that I had avoided a possible indecent exposure charge, when *quelle horreur*! the couple stopped, turned round and walked purposefully towards my car. The young lady tapped on my window, which I duly lowered as much as I dared, and asked if she might borrow my map for a minute, as she and her boyfriend had taken a wrong turning.

I would like to ask for the young lady's forgiveness – under normal circumstances I would have not said 'No' and driven off at speed leaving her lost and perplexed. And most of all, I am sorry about her boyfriend's foot, which seemed to be underneath my front wheel! I'm quite sure they will forgive me when hearing the explanation of what was under the map! But I'm not too sure about Dianne.

Yours sincerely, and hoping for absolution,

Barry.

Dear Simon,

As you may guess from my name, I am Welsh, but of late, our rugby team has been rather good at coming second. The incident for which I require forgiveness occurred some two years ago when Wales visited 'H.Q.' at Twickers to play against England.

I was living in the West Country at the time, and 15 of us acquired tickets for the big match. We decided to make a day of it, and arranged a game of rugby for the morning against one of the London teams. We also hired a mini-bus that had seen better days for the journey. However, the normal two-hour journey took twice as long, and, as we were running late, we decided to change on the bus, exposing ourselves to all and sundry.

We ran onto the field of battle, and within five minutes the only other Welshman on the field had been sent off for foul play. This was not to be our day! We got well and truly stuffed by the opposition, only to troop down the road and see Wales similarly humiliated. I was initially magnanimous in defeat, taking all the leg-pulling about Wales's defeat in my stride. However, during the traditional arm-bending session that followed, I began to tire of the constant jibes.

At closing time, we retired to a local curry shop to finish the night in style. We rearranged the restaurant furniture so that we could all sit together on one long table, emptying the establishment of its regular Saturday night clientele in the process. I ordered a pleasantly mild dish and went to answer the call of nature. Upon my return, the meal arrived and I took my first mouthful. My head nearly exploded, as during my absence my order had been changed by my fellow revellers to the hottest spicy dish on the menu, a chicken phall. I should have been suspicious, as the dish was surrounded by six raw chillies.

I could not eat another mouthful, and I was subject to further ridicule, for not only had my team lost, but I was not man enough to finish my meal. A guy called Jim Green took pity on me and, to great applause, he finished my curry without any apparent ill-effects, though he wisely left behind the six chillies.

I had suffered enough for one day and planned my revenge. I acquired a mild green pepper and sliced it up into segments that, from a distance, resembled the chillies. To regain some respect for myself and my nation, I challenged Jim to a chili eating contest, which he foolishly accepted. I ate my green pepper, Jim ate all six chillies. I had never seen a human chameleon before – Jim's hue changed from red to yellow to white to ashen and finally to match his surname, green, all in a matter of minutes.

With some honour restored for my so-called chili-eating exploits, we got onto the bus for the journey home, but nobody had allowed for its rapid effect on the human digestive tract. We had to make several impromptu stops on the M4 for the unfortunate Jim, so the return journey took even longer than the outward one. My fellow travellers were truly amazed that I had not succumbed as Jim had. I was thus reinstated as a member of the 'real man' club, and deemed to be the winner of the competition.

I wish I could say this sorry tale stops at journey's end. Jim was employed by Her Majesty's Armed Forces and, as he could not prise himself from his commode for the following five days to take up his guard duty, my foolish competition placed the nation's security at risk! When, I next met Jim, he was understandably frosty towards me, for everybody was insistent that he paid for both his meal and mine.

Gareth.

9

Innocent Victims

It's the oldest gag in the book: man slips on banana skin, falls over and we laugh at his misfortune. So much humour seems to be based around other people's discomfort, it would be strange if we didn't have a chapter devoted to it.

Over the next few pages you'll find vindictiveness, pain, death, cruelty, humiliation, and grievous bodily harm. And you're laughing?

Dear Father Simon,

It is nearly ten years since my sin and I feel it is now time to own up, especially as the victim of the unfortunate circumstances no longer works for the BBC.

My true confession goes back to July 1981, the evening before Royal Wedding Day. Early that evening a large number of people travelled up to London from Dartford, the intention being that equipped with a life-sized wooden caricature of Prince Charles we would have a 'Royal Stag Night' on his behalf.

Things went mostly to plan and after a few hours it was clear that many other people had similar ideas. By about 8.30 pm the main group had moved to a hostelry in Covent Garden which has a balcony overlooking the square. As stragglers from our group arrived our youthful high spirits meant they had to dodge into the doorway to avoid spillages from the balcony above. I admit I was one of the perpetrators of the stupidity. However, what happened next was totally unintentional.

Immediately after that incident, everyone's attention was drawn to the square below. Standing in what was originally a light grey suit, now severely darkened by falling beer, was none other than television personality Frank Bough, accompanied by a couple of friends.

He was not too pleased and the situation was not helped by the roars of laughter now coming from the balcony and the square itself. Fortunately, after showing his displeasure Frank moved on.

So Simon, am I forgiven for the 'accident' born out of high intoxication and a nationalistic duty to help 'our' Prince Charles enjoy his stag night.

Mal.

Dear Father Simon,

This is the confession of a poor, neglected school lighting technician, who one day felt a little bit too poor and neglected and became ever so slightly vindictive.

I was lighting a choral concert at my school. One of the bosses was our senior master, who was blessed with an exceptionally bald head. To protect his identity, I shall refer to him as 'Dobber'. During the final rehearsal for this concert, I focused a couple of hundred watts of light onto his bonce. Within minutes, he was perspiring and patting his forehead with his hanky.

After the rehearsal, he endeavoured to change places with a neighbour. However, I noted which chair he placed his music on, and whilst everyone else was out getting changed for the performance, I focused several thousand watts on where his pate would be very shortly – including 500 watts on a tripod stand about a metre above where his head would be when he stood up.

The concert was about to begin. I kept all the lights at a very low intensity until the conductor came in and everyone took their places. I whacked the lights up to full power, and watched Dobber gently implode as he realized he was utterly utterly caught. The sweat was soon pouring off him. At the end of every piece, out came the handkerchief, dab dab dab, and it wasn't long before the audience were laughing as much as I was. (You couldn't miss him. He was lit up like Scotty was about to beam him up.)

After about an hour of this, I realized to my horror, that his skin was starting to peel. As I had wired all the lights onto a single circuit, I could not dim the lights on Dobber separately. There was nothing either of us could do. I sat there helpless, as Dobber sat there flaking.

Although I made myself very scarce after the concert, I overheard him making remarks about his grilling in his broad Welsh accent, 'Aawh! These lights seem to get me wherever I go!' For the next week or so, he had a very pink forehead, which, judging by the sound he made when anything came within a metre of it, was also very tender.

Sorry Dobber. Maybe it'll make your hair grow back.

Am I forgiven or should I just go and jump off Number 1 lighting bar with a 15-amp extension lead tied around my neck?

Anonymous.

Dear Simon and the rest of you,

We used to be three horrible teenagers and now we are three mature married women. However, we have decided that I should finally confess for all of us for ruining other people's happiness a long time ago.

Many many years ago we were at school in the north, the sort of school where every day was started with a short prayer and a hymn. As the vicarage was next door, the local vicar (not married, youngish and good looking but with absolutely no sense of humour!) used to trot over three or four mornings in a week to 'open the day'. We all were supposed to join singing the hymn, but most often the poor vicar was performing a solo unless our French teacher Mademoiselle Desvaux was there. Then it was a duet. Either way, utterly boring.

So the headmistress decided that boosting was needed and ordered that from then on the songs would be played from a tape through the central radio system and each teacher in turn was supposed to take care of finding suitable pious songs for a week. The radio/tape equipment was in the audio room which was used as a language laboratory and was normally locked. As Mademoiselle usually had her lessons there first in the morning, she normally had the key and therefore took care of switching on the tape after the prayer.

The hymns were blasted through speakers for a while but it was still utterly boring, so we decided to liven up the performance. We knew that Mademoiselle had set her eyes on the vicar thinking he would be a good catch, and the vicar was aware of it. We also knew that every morning after switching on the tape Mademoiselle slipped into the ladies' room to check her hair and makeup in case there was a chance for a little innocent chat with the vicar afterwards. So one day during the French lessons when it was Mademoiselle's week to choose the songs, I secretly pocketed the next morning's tape and replaced it with another one with an identical label.

Next morning the vicar gave his talk and stepped back nodding to Mademoiselle with a benevolent smile. She disappeared to the audio room flashing a radiant smile back at him. We waited. And dreamy music filled the hall, soon turning into something slightly embarrassing.

What we had chosen was a rather steamy French love song 'Je t'aime'. It was worth seeing how the benevolent smile soon started to fade from the vicar's face and he started to turn oddly pink.

The headmistress decided that it was enough and tried to get to the radio, but the door was locked. Mademoiselle was in the ladies' room totally unaware of what was going on, and by the time the caretaker was found with a set of keys, the song had finished. Mademoiselle came out and the vicar said: 'You have an unusual taste in music. Mademoiselle Desvaux' And she beamed back: 'Oh I am so glad you liked it, all songs this week are personally chosen by me and I always try to have a message in them.' At which point the vicar fled.

Poor Mademoiselle never found out why the vicar suddenly stopped coming, and one of us was quick to replace the original tape during the first lesson. She handed over her resignation at the end of term and went back to France. The vicar married a local nurse to the great relief of his parishioners, as they hadn't particularly fancied the idea of having a French mademoiselle as their vicar's wife.

Mademoiselle Desvaux, please forgive Jackie, Sara and Caroline for ruining your chances. We hope you have found happiness back home. And Simon, are we forgiven?

Yours faithfully,
Caroline.

Dear Simon,

This is a confession of a friend of mine from when we used to work together in a hotel. Every Saturday throughout the summer we had a contract with a coach company which brought pensioners from the North-east to the south coast for a summer holiday. As the hotel was situated in the Midlands, just two minutes from the M1, we were the ideal place to stop for lunch.

The coach company were pleased with the arrangements for we provided an excellent three-course meal with coffee at a reasonable price, and it did not seem to mind if the coach was delayed on route. The staff however did not feel the same way. The meal was more like musical chairs than a respectable lunch. After 20 minutes of deciding who was to sit where, over half of them remembered they wanted to go to the loo, and the others had left their teeth on the coach. Questions like 'Would you like any wine?' were often met with 'It's a quarter past two, lovey'. I must admit we did play on this slightly, like when asked by a respectable gent if he could have a gin and tonic for his wife, we would tell him, 'Sorry, we don't do swaps'.

On this particular day, after the normal shuffle round, and the 'hold on, I want to sit next to Elsie' routine, we started to serve the soup. Cream of tomato, mmm lovely. As you probably know, waiters have a way of holding three soup bowls, two in one hand and one in the other. My friend leant round one lady to serve her soup, but when straightening up he noticed, to his surprise, the top bowl of the other two was empty. The red trace left in the bowl showed it had tipped out while he was serving the first. He looked down and saw it had poured, quite neatly into an open handbag. Without hesitation he did what all well-trained waiters do – he said nothing and shut the bag with his foot.

The rest of the meal went without a hitch, and we all lined up to watch the old biddies climb back aboard their coach, resisting the temptation to tap our soup smuggler on the shoulder, and arrest her for 'shoplifting'.

As a footnote, our record for serving the three courses and coffee, is 27 minutes. We only ever did this the once, for one lady fainted, two developed some type of shaking fit, and one sweet old man had a nose bleed.

All this happened over 15 years ago. Do you think the soup smuggler forgave us? Would you?

Michael.

Dear Father Simon,

Due to pressure from my girlfriend Gaynor, I've been forced to confess to something that happened about four years ago when I was a taxi driver in Birmingham.

It was a summer's day in Birmingham when I picked up a family from the airport. They were going to a posh area of Brum about 10 miles away. The older members of the family couldn't speak English very well, but the children could. They said they were going to a family reunion.

When I got them to their destination I got their cases out of the boot, opened the doors for them, helped them out, like a professional cabbie. Feeling very pleased with myself, I told them the fare was £12, not including the tip I thought I deserved. They paid me the fare plus a very small tip, I said thank you very much sir, and got back into the car. As I got in I noticed they had left something in the car. I picked it up carefully with my forefinger and thumb – it was a silk scarf wrapped round a small container.

I shouted at the gentleman telling him he forgot something. One of the children came up to the car. As I passed it out the window holding it with my forefinger and thumb the container fell to the ground spilling its contents in the gutter. I said to the young boy, 'sorry son was it valuable'? He replied, 'No it was my grandad', whose ashes were being blown down the street. I promptly drove off feeling very guilty.

I would like to apologize to this family for what happened. Can I ever be forgiven?

Yours faithfully,
Joe.

Dear Simon and the Crew,

I feel I must write to beg you for forgiveness. My confession happened in 1983 when I was working in a hairdressing salon.

The trend in hair fashions changed dramatically from long to short which, as you can imagine, is quite a big job and took quite a long time if performed by just using scissors. As it was a busy day and the appointment system restricted to 30 minutes I decided to take a short cut (no pun intended) and use clippers with a restricted guard.

As I took the clippers through the hair shedding the long locks it happened! The clippers appeared through the masses of hair but to my horror there was no guard to be seen. I panicked and frantically plucked the plastic guard from the hair. My apprentice looked on in amazement, with a smug grin, clearly thinking 'Get out of this one'.

As we had been chatting to this young man about how important first impressions were at interviews I knew he had just left school and was heading into the big wide world. Then it came to me 'Have you been worrying about anything?' I asked. 'No, I don't think so,' he replied. 'Have you just done your exams?' I questioned cautiously. 'Yes,' he said to my life saving relief. 'Why?' 'Well, you have a small bald patch on the back of your head!' I told him with concern, 'but don't worry. This sometimes happens during stressful times, such as studying or when under intense pressure. I wouldn't worry about it though it seems to be growing back as there is some stubble already there.' Little did he know that my unguarded clippers had created this stress-ridden bald patch.

This 16 year-old man continued to visit the salon and we eventually managed to disguise the patch. He told me he did not get the job for which the important haircut was requested, I feel guilty about this unfortunate accident every day.

Please find it in your hearts to forgive so I can forget. I work for a large hairdressing cosmetic company as a trainer, and this young man will be 24 by now and I don't fancy coming face-to-face with a six-foot revenge-ridden guy.

Thanks and regards,
Gary.

Dear Simon,

I want to confess about something that has been playing on my conscience for over 30 years now, and as a last resort I am turning to you for help, for I feel that by sharing my guilty secret with you, I may find it easier to live with in future.

It all started when I was a 16 year-old lad, and was working for the Post Office as a messenger boy, in the building that used to be the head office near St Paul's Cathedral. Our operations room was in the basement of the building, and there was a strict rule that smoking was prohibited in the whole of the basement area. However, the cleaners had their lockers in the basement, not far from our room, and had positioned all these lockers in a square so that no-one could see inside. They would use this area for their tea breaks and there was always much noise and music coming from within, day and night. Whenever any of us tried to look behind the screens, we were always greeted with shouts of abuse and scorn, for invading the secrecy of this private place. For us young lads, it was very hard to pass this mysterious place by without first trying to obtain a glimpse of what was happening within.

One morning I arrived at work for the early shift, and, as usual, loud music was coming from behind the lockers. As I walked past I could see there were clouds of smoke coming up over the top of the lockers. Then I noticed some fire buckets hanging on the wall next to me. Suddenly, I was overcome with an uncontrollable urge I cannot explain. Yes, you guessed it, I looked inside the fire buckets, two had sand inside, and two had water; I took hold of one of the water buckets, shouted 'Fire' at the top of my voice, and threw it over the top of the lockers.

The water went over in one large lump, and, as I turned and ran for my life, I heard unimaginable screams and wails behind me. I ran to the operations room and locked myself in the toilet. My heart was beating so fast I thought it would burst, but after a few minutes I plucked up courage to go back outside, and walked back to the place where the incident happened, whistling innocently. There was a crowd of people around someone on the floor, and as I melted into the background, I heard what had happened. Just after I disappeared around the corner, a postman happened to walk past as a very large West Indian cleaner ran out from behind the locker soaked from head to toe. He hit the postman square between the eyes, knocking him unconscious, and then proceeded to kick him for doing this ghastly deed.

By the time the ambulancemen arrived the postman was conscious again and protesting at an unprovoked attack. He was taken to hospital with head injuries, and shortly after that, my legs turned to jelly as the police arrived. The cleaner protested that the postman had deliberately drenched him with water, and was eventually taken away to the police station.

I want to convey my sincere apologies to both these people and I assure them that the guilt I have felt over these years must be far greater than any hurt I may have caused them. I feel this episode must have been a great lesson in life for each of us, albeit for different reasons.

Thank you,
Dave.

Dear Crew,

Whilst at college in Durham I played American Football for the Washington Grays (if the London Monarchs would like to make an offer for me I will play for half of Ellery Hanley's wages). We had a very successful season in 1989 progressing to the Division 1 semi-finals against the Cheltenham Chieftains.

The lads stayed in Cheltenham the night before, and like true Geordie boys they rampaged the town, dropping trousers, beating up bouncers and sinking boats on the boating lake. The next day almost everyone was feeling rough, after not returning to the hotel until 3 am.

The game commenced and Cheltenham chewed us up and spat us out. At 44−8 down late in the game our quarterback threw an interception. Everybody converged around the ball and a bit of barging started. I was really fed up after just missing the final for the fourth successive year. As a reflex I walked up to one of their players, a monster 6'2" (and a very good player) full of muscles, who had been giving me a rough time all day. Being only 5'7" my head was at the level of his shoulder pad. As I walked past I brushed by head against his shoulder and threw myself to the ground, writhing in a dazed agony.

The referees, our players and fans saw me slump, mortally wounded. This really got people incensed. The fans shouted for the 'Thug' to be sent off, the players started scrapping, the referees were in a panic trying to calm everyone down whilst the physio was giving me smelling salts and asking me to count his fingers.

Anyway the innocent thug was sent off, and I was consoled on the sideline.

We still lost.

I went to the final the following week to pick up an award as the league top receiver. There on the sideline was this poor dejected chap, suspended from the final, a British National Final, something very few people manage to get to in a lifetime, something I've failed to get to in seven attempts.

Cheltenham did win the final, despite being short of one of their star players.

So I would like you to absolve me and the player I bounced off to forgive me.

A very humble,
Darren.

Dear Simon Mayo,

I am 19 years old. I feel I must confess to an incident that took place when I was only 16 and at my secondary school. At the time I had, what I thought were special feelings towards the English master at my school. His name was Mr P. I got it into my head that he liked me a lot by the way that he would smile at me. He was much older than me but I still couldn't help feeling deep stirring at the bottom of my soul whenever he started to talk about grammar.

Bearing this in mind I cannot help feeling guilty for what happened at one of the schools Christmas discos. As usual the disco was boring. The music was old and there were not many lights, and so there were only a few people on the dance floor. I built up a little courage and went up to ask Mr P. whether he would dance with me. I didn't expect him to say yes, but he did. We danced for a bit and he was smiling as usual. After a while, Mr P. had to leave the dance floor because some boys had been found smoking in the changing rooms. I followed him out, and after he had dealt with the smokers he went into the changing room, I presume, to see everything was intact. I crept in to the changing rooms, and turned the key which he had left in the door. He sprung around at the noise of the key turning, and gave a startled yelp. 'Oh, its you Sally' he said, 'what do your want?'

Well, I thought that I would dive in at the deep end and so I asked him whether he liked me or not. He replied with an 'Eh What?' I could see he was confused, so I repeated the question. When what I was saying had sunk in, instead of answering me in any way he said something along the lines of 'Well got to go', and made a spring for the door. He reached it and found it was locked, with the air of a criminal, who, standing in front of a firing squad, finds his bindings loose, only to discover someone has just shouted 'Aim . . . Fire'. Agitated is the word I'm looking for. He turned around and as I saw his eyes darting around the room for other escape routes I felt embarrassed and kind of let down. I lost what might be called my marbles for an instant.

Mr P. must have seen something in my eyes, because he was backing off rapidly, and, with the heat of the moment and all that, I gave chase. The confines of my old school changing rooms were small to say the least, and as we approached the eighth or ninth lap and last bench hurdle a key turned in the door and their stood the school janitor. Because the room is small, and Mr P. had got a good lead under starters orders, it looked to this janitor as though Mr P. was chasing me. This janitor was a righteous bod, and wouldn't stand for any of that kind of thing, and so he reported it to the headmaster immediately. Mr P. got suspended for three weeks without pay because I was so embarrassed I wouldn't speak up.

I confess all now, however, and I would just like to say sorry to Mr P. and say to the headmaster involved that I think three weeks was a bit stiff.

Am I forgiven?

Sally.

Dear Simon,

Last October, I met a rather attractive young lady, called Sonia, at my local pub. We got talking and found we got on very well. She told me she had a boyfriend, who was working away, so I knew where I stood from the start. I told her I had my own computer software company (and that, basically, I was loaded), so that she thought she knew where she stood. In fact, I'm a trainee Cost & Management Accountant, who has access to computers (occasionally) but that's a red herring. I'm not confessing that. (Should I, okay, stick it on the list, then.)

Anyway, for six weeks, I thoroughly enjoyed myself (if you know what I mean . . . I think you do!). Then one night, shortly before Christmas, Sonia phoned me, in a bit of a state, to say it was all off. Although I'd sort of expected it, I was still a little disappointed not to be able to see this nubile young goddess again. I comforted myself with the thought that, at least, I could now drop the pretence (and expense!) of being the successful self-made man and save myself a fortune on a Christmas present at the same time. My self-satisfaction lasted about three seconds.

Sonia went on to say that she hadn't been totally up front with me (I could hardly complain, could I?). Her boyfriend hadn't been working away at all. He had been residing at Her Majesty's Pleasure, on a charge of G.B.H. – his third charge of G.B.H. The news got steadily worse. Sonia had told him everything (and I do mean everything) that had gone on between us, during her last visit and he had, apparently, indicated his displeasure with the situation by threatening to tear my head off. Trying to remain calm, I explained that there would be nothing to worry about, as long as she didn't give him my name . . . oh . . . she already had . . . I was as good as dead.

For a fortnight, I hardly ventured from home, going to work only occasionally and never going out at night, not even to my local. As Christmas approached (the season of good-will and all that), I began to feel a bit safer as nothing had happened and no one had been in touch to say a psychopath had been making enquiries about me. Feeling the need to escape from the four walls surrounding me, I nipped down to the local for a 'swift pint'. One pint extended to two and, as I was about to sit down with my third, I glanced at the door to see a denim-clad, muscle-bound, tattooed, snarling, giant of a man enter the pub and make his way through the crowd. This was clearly no ordinary run-of-the-mill bar-room brawler, but the sort of man who gives violent, psychotic criminals a bad name. And, most importantly, it was the sort of man who fitted exactly Sonia's description of her boyfriend, Andy.

He approached two drinkers on the table next to me, mentioned my name and asked if they knew me. They weren't regulars and said they'd never heard of me, bless 'em. Next, Andy came over to me. I stood and looked into his piggy eyes, wondering what it felt like to spend six months in traction, which was obviously what the immediate future held for me. I was just about to feign a heart attack (with the minimum of acting), when Andy asked me the same question. In a flash, I saw a possible way to avoid the traction, at least for the time being. I looked round the pub until I saw the kind of chap who looked as though he might have his own successful computer software company. 'Yes,' I replied, trembling like a leaf, 'There he is at the bar . . . the one with the leather jacket and gold bracelets.'

Not even bothering to say 'Thanks', Andy strode past me. Whilst making my 'Sharp Exit', I heard the smashing of beer glasses and the screams of alarmed young women, as the Exocet hit its target. I sprinted home, not once looking back, sat down in a chair and carried on trembling until the sound of police car sirens in the distance restored some feeling of security.

The local newspaper eventually went some way to satisfying my curiosity as to what happened in the pub that night. Apparently, Andy's victim seems to have got off pretty lightly. He suffered only mild concussion, a broken nose and collar-bone, and cuts and bruises. Andy was duly arrested by about half a dozen extremely brave policemen. He is currently being held on remand, on an unrelated charge. By all accounts, he faces a pretty lengthy stretch this time, hence my apparent bravery in making this confession.

I would like to beg forgiveness from Andy's victim, for all the pain and suffering I caused him, when his only crime was to wear a leather jacket and a bit of gold jewellery.

   Please Simon, can you grant me absolution?

Yours remorsefully,
Dave.

10

Famous for Fifteen Minutes

99.9 per cent of all confessions are from people you've never heard of, never met, and probably never want to meet. But just occasionally, a famous person pops up, and we relish the dénouement even more.

So, Prince Philip, Jeremy Beadle, Her Majesty the Queen, Ricky Ross, Jimmy Hill, Paul Gascoigne and The Searchers, skip on to the back cover now. The rest of us can just smirk.

Dear Simon,

On 15th May 1990 I attended the relaunch of Roy of the Rovers magazine at the International Suite at White Hart Lane. The guest of honour, Paul Gascoine, was delayed due to his new Lotus breaking down on the M1 just outside Darlington. When he finally arrived, some four hours late, the remnants of the press corps – one reporter from the Romford Gazette – wanted pictures of him kicking a ball around on the Tottenham pitch.

Since there was no one else around I reluctantly volunteered to assist and, somewhat overawed by the experience, kicked the ball rather hard and low at 'our hero'. Paul stretched to reach the ball and in doing so, because he was so stiff from the long drive and wait on the motorway, pulled a stomach muscle.

Yes, Simon, it is I who was to blame for the much-publicized groin injury to the nation's favourite footballer. Until now I have been unable to share the gruesome truth, but now that Paul is completely recovered I feel able to accept the blame for everything that has befallen the greatest team on earth this season.

Am I forgiven Simon, and, if so, can you get me tickets for the match?

Yours sportingly,
Graeme.

Dear Father Mayo,

Back in the summer of 1984 when the miners strike was at its height, a friend and I decided impulsively to holiday in Scotland.

Not being too knowledgeable on the geography of the highlands, we headed for the Isle of Skye in my friend's car. All began well, although the drive to Skye seemed much longer than the maps indicated – long windy roads around long lochs and sprawling mountains that went on and on and on. However, we did manage to catch the last ferry from Kyle of Lochalsh across to Skye – only to discover that all bed and breakfast accommodation on the island was already occupied. We ended up sleeping a very rough night in a small car on the side of the A863. Not to be recommended.

After a further night in Skye, we decided to move on. We headed up the West Coast towards Ullapool in no particular hurry. That is, until my friend hit upon the idea of driving around the perimeter of Scotland. What a great idea, we thought. We had three remaining days, and if we drove several hundred miles a day we could complete our journey with time to spare on the way!

We agreed to give it a go. Why not? As we continued up and up the coastal roads, we began to realize that if our goal was to be achieved we would have to put our foot down. This is where the fun began! As we drove faster and faster, taking the corners on the wrong side of the road, dodging other cars and swerving to miss sheep on the open roads, we began to understand the appeal of 'Scotland's for Me!'. We would each take our turn in driving – each trying to scare the one another with ever-increasing feats of risky courage.

On one remote stretch (where we hadn't passed a car in 10 miles) I took one corner a little wider than even we were used to. We narrowly avoided a cliffside drop. Before returning to my side of the road, a large black limousine with gold flags came around the corner. Both swerving to avoid each other, the limo came off worse, but we recovered our direction and continued on.

Shortly afterwards we drove across a large viaduct-like bridge which seemed very new. In fact it was. People stood and clapped as we finished passing over it. A marquee was erected and large crowds were gathered. In our honour perhaps? We thought no more of the matter.

Later that evening in our bed and breakfast accommodation, we were shocked and horrified to see Her Majesty The Queen open the very same new bridge we had crossed earlier, before getting into her large black limousine with gold flags on, and driving off over the bridge.

My friend and I were now choking on our evening meal both thinking what each of us was fearing! Feeling uncomfortable at the prospect of being identified as endangering the life of our Monarch (especially as we were both HM civil servants at the time), we imagined terrible headlines and the awful prospects! Just then TV footage showed our car speeding across the bridge from the direction the limo had just gone in.

We made a hasty exit from our B & B and, indeed, Scotland. Please can you find it in your hearts to forgive us? I hope Her Majesty and the people of Scotland can too, as I would love to tour again (only this time at a speed where I can sightsee).

I wish to remain anonymous for obvious reasons, as I do not wish to end my days in the Tower.

Yours recklessly,
Alias John Smith.

Dear Father Simon,

I would like not only to confess – but to apologize – for something that happened about five years ago. I'd just come back from holiday in Corfu where I met a guy called George who came from Edinburgh. We met one drunken night when he rescued me from a 10-foot hole – but that's another story.

We got on like a house on fire – so when he invited me up to Edinburgh for the weekend – I thought a brief repeat of our holiday would go down a treat. Well, he was a big Hibs fan – and we were going to see the Hibernian v Heart of Midlothian game on Saturday. I was sure that I'd be able to hold my own in the bar and show those Scots how real Englishmen knock back the booze – a real intellectual's weekend, you see.

After two hours in the pub the match passed into oblivion. Another two in the pub afterwards and four bags of chicken crisps didn't help my condition, but as the licensing laws in Scotland are so generous, we didn't even have to go home and wait for the pubs to re-open. We began our evening session there and then.

In one pub a band were frantically playing to a crowd of about 100 people – but I was beyond any musical appreciation at that stage of the evening. I was only interested in drooling over a few girls who were in such a state they no longer had any discerning taste and didn't mind my leering. One poor girl was receiving my attentions in a big way when I suddenly began to feel very queasy and had to excuse myself. She wasn't keen to let me go and held on – I started to panic – boy, did I need to get out for some fresh air or something drastic was going to happen very soon.

Each time I stepped away she grabbed me tighter around the stomach – which was I have to say – a really bad move!! In the end I shoved her away and stumbled to the door. Because the band was playing, people were packing the floor area and I couldn't wade my way through them. Things were looking decidedly dodgy at this point for I really needed to get outside quick. My escape route only seemed to be if I pushed down to the front and by the stage where the band were playing. As I got halfway along just to where the band's frontman was giving his all – the 20 pints of lager and bags of crisps took its toll, and I was sick.

Unfortunately – and to my utter embarrassment – my aim was not clever and the vomit ended up all over the singer's shoes. As I turned and legged it away back to my new-found girl, I could see some poor lad being dragged from the front of the stage and thrown out into the street by a big burly bouncer – someone you wouldn't really bother protesting your innocence to.

I'd got off scot-free (if you pardon the bad pun), but it isn't for this that I'd like to apologize. The poor singer who had his shoes sprayed while he was desperately trying to impress the crowd was no other than the then – struggling singer, Ricky Ross, with his band Deacon Blue.

Sorry Ricky, but I reckon that by now you'll be able to buy yourself a new pair of shoes.

Mark.

Dear Father Simon,

Unlike some of your confessions, the one I am about to relate took place not several years ago, or even several months ago. It took place today, and I must confess and get it off my chest immediately.

Security reasons forbid me revealing the exact location where this incident took place, but just say it was somewhere in rural Lancashire. Tired of motorway driving, I was heading home from work along a little-used country lane when I came upon a group of men wandering about in the middle of the road ahead of me. The men were obviously 'country types', dressed as they were in waxed jackets and green wellies. Gun dogs were much in evidence, as were braces of grouse and pheasant strung about their shoulders. These 'country types' were evidently coming off the moors at the end of a day's huntin' and a-shootin' and were getting into various Land Rovers parked at the roadside.

Feeling in a bit of a bolshie mood I thought to myself, 'Come the revolution all this cruelty and privilege will be over', as one idly does, when I unwittingly came mighty close to kicking off the aforementioned revolution myself.

At the approach of my car, the men parted to allow me through. But not all of the men ... rounding a bend, three were still in the road. Two of them wandered to the side, the third however, did not. Thinking he may be a bit deaf, I was about to sound my horn when the gentleman concerned turned round. Seeing my car for the first time he was forced to dash to the side of the road with a genuinely startled look on his face.

Startled look or not I recognized this man straight away and thanked my lucky stars I hadn't had time to honk my horn. It is for startling this particular man that I lay my guilt before a shocked nation in the hope of forgiveness. If the gentleman concerned is reading this, I apologize most profusely to you, sir, and hope you can find it in your heart to forgive me, your Royal Highness, Prince Philip.

Yours, prostrate with guilt and apoplectic with apology,

Paul.

P.S. Please write to me c/o the Tower of London Dungeons where I shall no doubt be incarcerated soon.

Dear Father Mayo,
This confession goes back to the football season of 1990, when Cambridge United were playing at home to Fulham. I was at that time a member of the Special Constabulary, which meant I usually got the wonderfully boring job of directing the traffic outside the football ground. However, this ensured I was rarely given a job within the stadium itself and was able to watch the game and drift round all the Hot Dog stalls, claiming a free cup of tea from each of them.

On this occasion I was having a particularly bad time with the motoring public. This wasn't being helped by the fact that the regular policemen found it more amusing to watch me waving my arms frantically at the oncoming cars than to give me a hand in the road. The start of the game drew closer, the traffic and pedestrians increased, as was to be expected, and the number of people asking for directions to the car park grew to an unbearable level.

I signalled to the next lot of cars to proceed and upon drawing level with me, the first car stopped and wound down the window. There were a couple inside. The man stuck his head out of the window and asked, 'Excuse me, could you direct me to the car park?' Surprised by the unusual politeness of this football supporter, I gave him the instructions where to go. I said it seemed a long way from the stadium but in fact it brought you out the other side of the ground and about five minutes' walk from the away supporters end. The man thanked me and drove away. About 10 minutes later the same couple drew up next to me. The man was not so polite this time and told me I had just sent him on a wild goose chase. This I was not too happy with and so, glaring at him from under my peaked hat, I told him the car park was exactly where I said it was and proceeded to give him the instructions again. As he drove off up the road a second time, I suddenly remembered where I had seen his face before. It was Jimmy Hill and, as I later found out, his newly wed wife. I also found out later that Jimmy Hill is a director of Fulham and therefore allowed to park in the Directors' car park.

Oh well, I am not a great follower of the sport so how was I to know?

Another 10 minutes passed and guess who should appear again, yup, my friend Jimmy and he was even less amused than last time. So again I gave him the directions, although I think a new pair of glasses would have been more appropriate. Off he trundled for the third time, only to reappear for a fourth and fifth time, getting more annoyed each time he found his way back to the front of the football ground. This was all too amusing for me, for the game was just about to begin and he had still not managed to park. As I was unaware of Jimmy's affiliation with the opposing team, I could only imagine he had turned up to do some commentating, for which he was now going to be late.

Jimmy Hill seemed to be getting very hot under the collar, as the game was up and running by now. I told him that due to the match starting, there would no longer be a policeman on the common and the gate would have been locked to stop cars from being stolen. Therefore he would have to find a nearby road to park in. There was,

however, a slight problem — all the roads would either have been parked in by those in the know, or would have 'No Parking' cones placed along the verge.

Hoping he would park on a coned-off road, I left my post to watch the match and have numerous cups of tea. It was my intention to go out of the ground at half-time, find his car and put a parking ticket on it. However, he managed to find a place to park legally and so I called it a day.

The burden of the foregoing forced me to resign from the Special Constabulary, but if the powers that be were to have found out about this while I was still enlisted, I'm sure I would have been kicked out. I therefore wish to be forgiven by Jimmy Hill for undoubtedly spoiling his honeymoon, which he was in the middle of, and ruining the start of the match for him. Cambridge United ruined the rest of the game for him by winning.

I also apologize for wasting so much of his petrol in making him drive round the block so many times. However, all my instructions on how to get to the car park were correct, so how he managed to miss it, God only knows.

Yours in need of forgiveness,
Henry.

Dear Sir,

I seek forgiveness for a most unworthy and deplorable act which has plagued me for some 40 years.

In 1941 I was a 17-year-old laboratory assistant working for the Ministry of Defence. I had been employed by the government to work with a team of scientists who were developing a serum which would win us the war. Their aim was to produce a serum which, when mixed in water, would promote docile and apathetic behaviour in the recipient. A main ingredient was a hormone that promoted childish behaviour by suppressing various fears that mature people possess.

The work was slow and laborious and had just reached the final stage, where we were to use human guinea pigs in the form of prisoners of war, when the war ended. Our department suddenly became an embarrassment to the Government and so we were disbanded and the serum destroyed. All, that is, bar one small ampoule I 'mistakenly' slipped into my pocket on our last day. Can you blame me? I had worked day and night for years on the project and then suddenly I was told all my work was for nothing and I was not to mention it to anyone else ever again.

However, it is not the theft of the small ampoule for which I seek forgiveness. A few years later I was living next door to a very pleasant couple who seemed intent on rearing what can only be described as a demonic child called Jerry. Every day I would find dead birds in my garden that Jerry had shot with his air pistol. Old ladies feared to walk the streets lest he should charge them down on his bicycle.

One morning, whilst helping another pensioner-victim of Jerry to her feet, I decided it was time the serum was tested on a human guinea pig. Administering the drug was no problem. I simply dissolved it in a bottle of fizzy-pop, which I then left on the window sill in my kitchen and left the window open. Sure enough, within half-an-hour a little hand removed the full bottle and seconds later replaced the bottle duly emptied.

I will regret that day for the rest of my life. At first there were no obvious effects and Jerry continued to behave like a little monster. I believed the serum to be a failure. However as the years rolled on I realized what an awful mistake I had made. Outwardly Jerry grew as any normal human being, but mentally he remained a seven-year-old with the same malicious streak. Indeed, the older he gets the more warped he becomes.

And so I would ask forgiveness from yourself for recklessly administering serum ZXT123.5 all those years ago and through my actions burdening the world with . . .

JEREMY BEADLE!!

Yours faithfully,
Dr Gordon.

P.S. Please withhold address for M.O.D. reasons.

P.P.S. I am currently working on a project whereby we cross Bernard Matthews with an Essex Girl to create the perfect Gobbler!

Dear Father Simon,

My story goes back to the 'swinging sixties'. My best friend, Brenda, and I were avid fans of anything and anyone remotely musical.

Being poor teenagers with a pittance for pocket money we didn't often get the chance to see the groups 'live', so we contented ourselves with trying to get autographs to flash around at school in order to amaze and impress our friends.

One day we noted with interest that quite a few famous groups were due to appear the next night at The Odeon, so we vowed to go autograph hunting.

We were quite successful that afternoon and managed to get The Zombies' autographs (they were quite a famous group at the time), but the real scoop would be to try and get the Searchers (of Needles and Pins fame), but alas to no avail. We pledged to return that evening and renew our efforts, which we did.

We also met a 'youth' who took quite a shine to me. We soon began to realize our mission would not bear any fruit because we had got to be in by 9.30 pm and the show didn't finish until quite a bit later. Our new friend sensed our disappointment and promised to show us where The Searchers' van was parked. The 'youth', who was out to impress, said he would get me something better than their autographs, and produced a hacksaw and promptly presented me with the van handle.

I was thrilled and went home triumphant. My Dad, however, was not impressed and, having given me a 'thick ear', made me see the error of my ways. I offered to send the handle back through the post anonymously, but he said they would trace my fingerprints. I believed him, so I hid it.

I would just like to apologize to The Searchers, who tried to get away from all the screaming fans, only to find they couldn't open their van door because the handle was missing. I know this is true because amongst the screaming mob were some girls from school who told me the story the next day. Of course I couldn't say I had the handle, so all in all it was a hollow victory.

Am I forgiven?

Chris.